Mace checked in on Zurie again. She was knocked out cold.

An hour later, he was showered, shaved and dressed in a casual long-sleeve black pullover and dark jeans. If Zurie wasn't alert enough to drive, he'd take her home. He still had plenty of time to drop her off and get to the precinct to change into his uniform before the start of his shift.

In the living room, Zurie snuggled into the pillow and mumbled in her sleep. From the smile on her face, she was having a really good dream. Too bad he had to wake her. Crashing on his couch for the night while he was at work was an option, but knowing her, she'd refuse.

Mace leaned down and shook her gently by the shoulder, but she didn't wake up. Not wanting to startle her, he spoke softly. "Zurie."

Blinking sleepily up at him, she laid her palm to his chest. Her lips parted with a sigh. "Mace..."

Zurie raised her head, slid her hand up to his nape and kissed him.

* * *

TILLBRIDGE STABLES:
These ranchers are roping horses—and hearts!

Dear Reader,

Thank you for choosing *The Cowgirl's Surprise Match* as your new escape into the world of love and happily-ever-after.

The responsibility of running Tillbridge Stable and Guesthouse is one Zurie Tillbridge has taken on with pride. Her accomplishments are many. But the work of maintaining her family's legacy hasn't been easy.

When she decides to take a few weeks off for rest and relaxation, as well as to help plan her cousin's secret wedding, the last thing she expects is Mason "Mace" Calderone coming into her life. As Mace challenges her belief that maintaining her family legacy and having fun can't coexist, Zurie gives him a new definition of home.

Embracing the good of home and family, in all its unexpected forms, and enjoying special moments and the people who are a part of them are things Zurie and Mace learn in this story. I must admit, they reminded me of the importance of those things in my own life. I love it when characters teach me a thing or two!

I also love hearing from readers. Instagram, Facebook and my newsletter are three of my favorite places to connect. You can also find out more about me and the books in the Tillbridge Stables series, as well as upcoming stories connected to them, at ninacrespo.com.

Zurie and Mace are waiting for you. Sit back, relax and join them on their journey to finding love.

Wishing you all the best!

Nina

The Cowgirl's Surprise Match

NINA CRESPO

HARLEQUIN®
SPECIAL
EDITION™

Recycling programs for this product may not exist in your area.

ISBN-13: 978-1-335-40467-1

The Cowgirl's Surprise Match

This edition published by arrangement with Harlequin Books S.A.

For questions and comments about the quality of this book, please contact us at CustomerService@Harlequin.com.

Harlequin Enterprises ULC
22 Adelaide St. West, 40th Floor
Toronto, Ontario M5H 4E3, Canada
www.Harlequin.com

Printed in U.S.A.

Nina Crespo lives in Florida, where she indulges in her favorite passions—the beach, a good glass of wine, date night with her own real-life hero and dancing. Her lifelong addiction to romance began in her teens while on a "borrowing spree" in her older sister's bedroom, where she discovered her first romance novel. Let Nina's sensual contemporary stories feed your own addiction for love, romance and happily-ever-after. Visit her at ninacrespo.com.

Books by Nina Crespo

Harlequin Special Edition

Tillbridge Stables

The Cowboy's Claim
Her Sweet Temptation

Visit the Author Profile page
at Harlequin.com for more titles.

Chapter One

Zurie Tillbridge opened the digital planner on her phone knowing exactly what to expect—“busy” written in bold letters across every day of the week.

As she scrolled through the tasks necessary to keep Tillbridge Horse Stable and Guesthouse at its best, her heartbeat consumed her chest and a small wave of burning unease churned the coffee she’d drunk earlier that morning in her stomach. The slightly off feeling had plagued her for over a week. She never got sick, not even with the common cold. What was going on?

Unbuttoning the navy blazer of her business suit, she sank into the beige chair and smoothed back a strand of her long black hair from her overly warm brown cheek. As the welcome cool air in her physician's private office seeped through her white blouse, she closed her eyes a moment, shutting out the slightly cluttered wood desk in front of her and the abstract paintings with splashes of orange hanging on the cream walls.

The side door opened, and Dr. Lily Westin walked in. Crisp and serene in a white lab coat, the midthirties brunette with a rosy complexion exuded energy.

Zurie waited until she sat down behind the desk. "So what's the verdict?"

"You'll live. I won't have your lab results for a couple of days, but my guess is your problems are stress and plain old exhaustion." Lily's green eyes held traces of humor and the candor of a friend. "What you need is a Mr. Tall, Hot and Irresistible in your life keeping you distracted so you'll stay where you belong right now—in bed, catching up on sleep."

A breath whooshed out of Zurie. *Whew!* She was just tired. But Lily's suggestion was hilarious. Even if she had time to lie around and do nothing, which she didn't, where would she find Mr. Tall, Hot and Irresistible in Bolan?

The image of a certain dark-haired guy flashed in her mind.

No way. Not him.

A laugh fueled another wave of relief as Zurie picked up her black designer tote from the chair beside her and put it on her lap. "That's an interesting diagnosis. Since Mr. Tall, Hot and Irresistible isn't available, are you giving me a B vitamin shot or a magic pill instead?"

"A shot or a magic pill won't do it. You need a break from Tillbridge."

"I have a stable and guesthouse to run."

"And you have capable people who can do more so you can do less."

"I can't." Zurie dropped her phone in her bag. "Especially now that there's a movie being filmed on the property."

Over the past few months, the filming of the sci-fi Western *Shadow Valley* had increased exposure and revenue for the stable, but it had also demanded more of everyone's time.

Lily leveled her gaze on Zurie. "Your body is trying to tell you something, and you need to start listening."

"Okay. I'll work on getting more sleep."

"What happens if Tillbridge loses you?"

Zurie's phone chimed in with a call, but the concern on Lily's face stopped her from answering it. "That would never happen."

"It could if you don't start taking better care of yourself." Lily got up and sat in the chair beside Zurie. "You're not eating properly. Your blood pressure is higher than it should be, and you're probably working on an ulcer. If you don't make some changes, there's a possibility the next time we have this conversation, you'll be in a hospital bed. You're only thirty-seven. You're too young to fall apart like this. Slow down before it's too late."

The voice mail alert pinged on Zurie's phone as Lily's words resonated. "You mean don't be like my dad."

Before her father, Mathew, had passed away, everyone had urged him to slow down, but he'd pointed to his full desk as the reason he couldn't.

Natural causes had been the official ruling. Some believed that as a widower, he'd worked himself into an early grave trying to hide from the pain of losing his childhood sweetheart, but still…

The image of her father burdened by stress wove through the tapestry of Zurie's memories like a too-bright thread, standing out. "If I had insisted he take time off, if I had begged, he might be alive today."

Lily lightly squeezing her arm alerted Zurie that she'd spoken aloud what she believed in her heart. "I know losing your father was a tough blow, but you can't blame yourself. No one knows what could have changed the past. I think the bigger question is, if your father were here right now, what would he tell you to do?"

Chapter Two

Zurie sat in the large brown leather chair that had once belonged to her father.

Sun from the window behind her glared off the financial spreadsheet displayed on the wide-screen computer on her desk. A few files and papers sat in the in-box on the left far corner of the desk while the out-box on the opposite side was full.

Not letting work pile up. Leaving nothing undone. That was her life as the co-owner of the stable. But today, for the first time in a long while, one uncertainty remained. The answer to the question Lily had asked her earlier that morning.

"What would he tell you to do?"

He'd tell her that Tillbridge had to come first. But if she didn't slow down and take a break as Lily suggested, she could end up letting down everyone who counted on her.

A knock at the door pulled Zurie from her thoughts. The meeting. She'd lost track of time. "Come in."

Her cousin Tristan, the stable manager and also a co-owner of Tillbridge, entered the office carrying his phone and a notepad. With his close-cut black hair and the strong angles of his brown face, he reminded her of their twin fathers, Mathew and Jacob.

From the faint smudges of dust on his standard work attire—black work boots, jeans and short-sleeved navy pullover—he'd come straight from the stable or one of the pastures.

He tipped his head toward the round meeting table on the other side of the room. "You ready?"

"Yes." Zurie took her padfolio from the left-hand drawer and grabbed her phone from the desk.

As she joined Tristan, she deciphered his slightly puzzled expression. She was usually already at the table, counting down the minutes to their 10:00 a.m. Wednesday meeting while squeezing in emails, calling her remote assistant, Kayla, and planning for the next meeting afterward.

Another knock sounded at the door and her sister, Rina, breezed in. "Good morning."

She laid her phone and keys on the table. Just like

Tristan, she had on jeans, plus she wore a lemon-yellow T-shirt with the white coffee cup logo and name of the café she owned, Brewed Haven. A matching headband held back her long braids, but the sunny color wasn't as eye-catching as the light of happiness in her brown eyes and the natural glow in her cheeks.

As Rina sat down, Tristan chuckled.

"What?" Rina shrugged at him. "Why are you looking at me? I'm not late."

"No reason. How long is he in town?"

She gave him a surprised look. "A couple of weeks. How did you know Scott was here? He flew in late last night."

Tristan winked at her. "Lucky guess."

Rina laughed. "How's Chloe?"

A huge smile took over his face. "She's great."

Feeling like the odd person out, Zurie opened her padfolio and powered up her computer tablet. A few months ago, when she'd made the last-minute deal with the movie production company to film *Shadow Valley* at Tillbridge, she'd never envisioned Tristan and Rina finding their significant others because of it.

Tristan had fallen for Chloe Daniels, one of the lead actors in the film, while Rina had gone head over heels for Scott Halsey, a stuntman who'd been a part of the crew until a knee injury had caused him to bow out.

Things were progressing in Tristan's and Rina's relationships. Soon they could both face a difficult choice—building their lives in California with the people they'd fallen in love with or staying at Tillbridge.

Images from her past she'd closed away about her own choices tried to get out. Zurie slammed the door shut. Tillbridge was more than enough to fill her life.

It was time to kick off the meeting. "Let's get started."

Zurie shared the information she'd received at the last chamber of commerce meeting in Bolan. An increase in tourism was anticipated later that year in the fall and winter months. Unfortunately, around the same time, major construction was planned on the primary road leading to Tillbridge, making the pothole-infested back road the main detour.

The route shift would surely deter the locals from visiting Pasture Lane Restaurant or holding events at the stable. Not to mention the bad impression it would make on the tourists. Luckily, at the mayor's weekly business mixer, she'd had a side conversation with him about it, and the mayor had promised to see if he could use his influence to change the order of construction to the back road being repaired first.

Tristan followed with an update on the stable and pasture management. The movie production was running behind. To accommodate the needs of the extended filming schedule, taking on new boarding and horse riding lesson clients was being delayed for at least four more weeks.

Rina took notes on her phone. Although she didn't participate in the day-to-day running of the stable, she was an equal third partner and still had a voice in the running of Tillbridge. "Are potential clients willing to wait that long or are we going to lose their business?"

"Most of them are willing to wait." Tristan sat back in the chair. "But no doubt we'll lose some of them."

"What if we offered an incentive?" Rina asked.

As Zurie worked through the financials of an incentive program in her mind, she couldn't stop a hand twitch. She missed her coffee. The caffeine jolt would have given her an energy boost and false comfort that she had the stamina to deal with the adjustments the film production was causing. But she had to lay off caffeine for a few weeks—doctor's orders.

As Rina and Tristan discussed possible incentives, Zurie remained in listening mode.

This time last year, their meetings had resembled a civil exchange between strangers instead of family. Actually, she'd been the stranger. Rina and Tristan had always gotten along. Lies and so many misunderstandings had nearly destroyed her relationship with them.

A few years ago, she'd believed Tristan had abandoned Tillbridge to pursue his bull-riding career, but then she'd learned about the sacrifices he'd made for their family. And with Rina—she'd failed to notice that her little sister didn't need her to resolve her problems anymore.

Memories of the illuminating and humbling conversations Zurie had had with Tristan and Rina over the past few months caused an internal wince. She'd been wrong about both of them, but it had been so easy to critique their actions and try to fix everything on her own.

As the oldest by five years over Tristan and almost ten years older than Rina, she'd often slipped into a parent-like role, especially when they were growing up. While her parents and her uncle, Jacob, who was Tristan's father, had handled business at Tillbridge, it had been her responsibility to get Tristan and Rina up and ready for school in the mornings and pack their lunches. At night, she'd helped them with their homework, and on weekends, when she wasn't practicing for the next barrel-racing competition or competing in one, she'd supervised them as they'd completed the small tasks they'd been assigned at the stable.

Sure, Tristan and Rina were adults now, but she still had the instinct to look out for them. Asking for more of their assistance at the stable so she could focus on improving her health felt…wrong. Tristan and Rina had experienced rough patches in their lives in the past, and now they were both so happy.

How could she do as Lily recommended without getting in the way of that and causing them to worry about her?

"I think those three incentives will work," Tristan said.

"I agree," Rina added. "What do you think, Zurie?"

Shoot! I missed everything they said. "I feel the same. As long as we keep an eye on expenses and continue to deliver top-notch customer service, we should be fine." Zurie closed her padfolio. "Unless there's anything else, I think we're d—"

A knock sounded at the door.

"Right on time." Tristan stood. "I asked someone to join us." He opened the door.

Chloe walked in, her dark curly hair bouncing near her shoulders. A similar glow to the one Rina had earlier lit up Chloe's pretty light brown face. Smiling next to Tristan in a fitted white T-shirt, skinny jeans, and high-heeled beige sandals, they were the perfect match as a couple.

He wrapped an arm around Chloe. "We have something important to tell you."

"Really?" Rina practically happy danced in her seat. "What?"

"We're engaged!" Tristan and Chloe said it at the same time as Chloe showed the sparkling diamond on her left hand.

Rina sprang from her seat. "Congratulations!"

She enveloped both of them in a hug, then turned to Chloe. "Girl, let me see that ring."

Zurie stood but hesitated in joining them, not quite sure where to interject herself into the moment.

Tristan's gaze met hers, and the happiness in his eyes was an irresistible invitation.

"Congratulations." Smiling, Zurie hugged Chloe first, then embraced Tristan. "So when's the big day?"

As Tristan said the date, he glanced to Chloe, confirming agreement, and she nodded.

"But that's just a little over six weeks from now," Rina said. "That's not a lot of time to plan a wedding."

"It is for a quick ceremony at the courthouse or in Vegas," Chloe responded. "When I'm done with studio work in California on *Shadow Valley*, I'm headed to Canada for my next production. Trying to juggle everything in our lives and plan a wedding is too much. And we don't want to wait."

"We don't need a big wedding." Love and pride shone in Tristan's face as he stared at Chloe. "She's agreed to become my wife. Nothing can top that." He briefly kissed her on the lips.

"But a wedding here would be so beautiful." Rina looked from Tristan to Chloe. "We can easily plan something small and intimate."

"We could." Chloe nodded. "But with the tabloids spreading false stories about me and the lead actor in the film being in a relationship, and paying for pictures and any scrap of news from the set, if we start planning a wedding, our personal life could be spun into some sort of crazy, jealous love triangle. We don't want that. We're even keeping our engagement a secret."

As Rina glanced down at Chloe's left hand, a glum expression took over her face. "So you won't get a chance to share the good news or show off that beautiful ring?"

"No." Chloe's gaze drifted to the platinum band with a marquis-cut diamond. "I'll have to keep this in my jewelry bag until we seal the deal at the courthouse or the twenty-four-hour chapel."

Chloe smiled, but Zurie caught the brief flash of sadness in her eyes. And the look of resignation in Tristan's.

He might not realize it now, but someday he would miss not seeing Chloe walk down the aisle. And they both might regret not sharing their vows with their family and close friends in attendance. But Tristan would take his disappointment to the grave to protect Chloe.

Before she could second-guess herself, Zurie let the words spill out. "It won't become a media circus if I'm making the plans instead of you."

Varying levels of doubt crossed Tristan's, Chloe's and Rina's faces.

"It's a lot of work..."

"We couldn't ask you to do that…"

"No. You're already doing too much…"

But the answer to Lily's question showed clearly in Zurie's mind. Her father would want her to make sure Tristan and Chloe had their big day. "Team Tillbridge."

The rallying cry her and Rina's father had used to motivate the family to get things done caught Tristan's and Rina's attention. The doubt in their faces melted slowly into smiles.

"Okay." Tristan nodded. "If you think we can team it out, I'm game."

Rina nudged his arm. "Of course we can."

Confused, Chloe looked at the three of them as if they'd suddenly started speaking a foreign language. "Team Tillbridge? Team it out? I don't understand."

Zurie reached out and squeezed Chloe's hand. "It means family takes care of family."

Chapter Three

In one efficient maneuver, Zurie parallel parked her gray Mercedes between two cars on Main Street. At seven forty-five on a Monday morning, the shops and residents in downtown Bolan were just starting to wake up. And she was beginning her first official day as Tristan and Chloe's wedding planner.

Five days ago, after she'd offered to handle the details of the ceremony and reception at Tillbridge, Tristan had insisted he take on more of her work as a trade. And then Rina had chimed in recommending Zurie take time off to work on the wedding and hand all her duties over to Tristan.

The remembered moment made Zurie smile. She

managed a horse stable and a guesthouse on a daily basis. How hard could one small wedding be? But seeing an opportunity to follow Lily's advice, she'd jumped on Rina's suggestion and feigned reluctance over taking time off. Then she'd bartered with them over how long she'd be out of the office. Otherwise they would have been suspicious. She hadn't missed a day of work in years. In the end, they'd settled on her taking three weeks off.

And they'd also decided to keep the engagement and the wedding a secret from mostly everyone until it happened. Tristan's birthday was a couple of weeks after the weekend he and Chloe wanted to get married. They could use that as an excuse to pretend that Zurie was helping Chloe plan an early "surprise" party for Tristan, since Chloe was leaving soon after filming of the movie ended.

Philippa Gayle, the guesthouse manager and executive chef of Pasture Lane Restaurant at Tillbridge, had been let in on the hush-hush ceremony. She'd agreed to cater the food for the reception and would handle most of the preparation herself.

Today's meeting at Rina's apartment above the café would start the ball rolling on ideas for the wedding cake Rina was going to make, as well as other ideas for the ceremony they would discuss later with Tristan and Chloe.

Zurie grabbed her black-and-blue animal-print bag from the passenger seat and got out. As she slipped the strap of the bag on her shoulder, she rounded the car and stepped onto the sidewalk. She joined the handful of dog walkers and joggers who were out for exercise and the employees heading to the shops linked together in strip-mall fashion that weren't open yet.

Sun glistened off water cascading down the stone fountain in the square located in the center of town. She would have cut through the space to reach the other side of the street, but workers mowed the grass around the benches and clipped pink and white flowering bushes lining the path.

A middle-aged jogger went around her without breaking his stride.

Maybe she should put running back onto her new healthy agenda. Years ago, she used to run three to five miles every other day. It would fit right in with not skipping meals, getting more sleep and enjoying time riding her horse, Lacy Belle. She'd even started meditating over the weekend…or at least she'd tried. Who knew breathing could be so darn challenging? She did it all the time.

Lily had suggested she try a variety of things to better her health, including a hobby. She'd never really had one of those. School, barrel racing and helping out where her parents needed her hadn't left time for much else. By the time she'd reached her mid-twenties, her focus had been finishing her master's degree in business and spending time with her father learning how to run Tillbridge.

Before she'd turned thirty, she'd been on a steep learning curve trying to catch up on all the things he hadn't gotten a chance to teach her. Trying to fit anything or anyone outside the stable into that equation had been impossible.

As Zurie walked past the ice cream shop near the left corner, the new manager, a dark-haired woman, gave her a quick smile before rushing into the establishment. The place had been sold, briefly closed for a few weeks and then reopened.

What was her name? She hadn't formally met the new manager yet. Tristan would probably be introduced to her at the mayor's business breakfast mixer at city hall that morning. She could find out the details about the manager and status of the ice cream shop from him. Wait. Tristan had said he couldn't make it this week. If she kept the wedding planning meeting to forty-five minutes, she could attend in his place.

A large pebble crunching underneath the sole of her low-heeled sandal drew Zurie's gaze downward. No, she couldn't go. Her jeans and short-sleeved peach-colored blouse were too casual for a professional gathering.

Fear of missing out started creeping in. She shoved it away. Aside from the wedding, her focus for the next few weeks was letting go of stress and taking in joy with every breath, like the beginner's meditation audio she'd listened to that morning had instructed.

She drew in a deep inhale, rich with the scent of freshly cut grass…and coffee.

Longing rose as she recalled the early-morning ritual of grinding her favorite blend of Colombian beans. Making the coffee in a French press and, when it was ready, pouring the steamy goodness into her A Yawn Is a Silent Scream For Coffee mug.

Disappointment pushed out an exhale. Drinking herbal tea, coffee's unfortunate step cousin twice removed, wasn't cutting it. She needed her caffeine fix. But she had to stick with the program. Her stomach was feeling better since she made the switch. Maybe the faint nagging headache she'd been experiencing lately, along with feeling jittery, would go away, too.

After waiting for cars to pass, she strode across the street toward Brewed Haven. Unlike the other businesses on the street, the two-story light-colored brick structure on the corner with large storefront windows on the first floor stood on its own.

A steady stream of customers entered and exited from the café with bags undoubtedly containing delicious pastries and cups filled with freshly brewed nirvana.

Thinking Zurie was headed inside, a friendly woman held the door open for her.

Suddenly, it was as if her feet had minds of their own and Zurie was propelled inside.

One small iced coffee wouldn't hurt. The one with extra whipped cream, chocolate sauce, caramel and a little sugar and sea salt sprinkled on top.

She slipped into the line leading up to the curved station.

Three baristas prepared coffees and grabbed desserts and pastries from the glass case underneath the counter.

When she placed her order, just saying the words *iced caramel mocha* gave her a caffeine-like buzz. Minutes later, the most beautiful creation ever to fill a clear plastic cup was in her possession.

Napkins. She'd better grab some. The cup was a little sticky. Weaving through the crowd, she made her way to the condiment station and snagged a few from the dispenser.

Taming the bag hanging from her shoulder with one hand while holding the iced coffee and napkins in the other, Zurie turned.

And smacked into a human wall.

Like a slow-motion scene in an action film, the clear domed top covering her cup of coveted mocha goodness came off, and iced coffee splashed up on a wide chest covered by a khaki-green athletic shirt.

Dang it. She hadn't even gotten a taste of her drink. Was it weird that she felt like crying about it?

She tipped back her head and looked up into the

naturally tanned face of Deputy Sheriff Mace Calderone. As she stared into his whiskey-colored eyes, Lily's cure flirted in her thoughts.

Tall...

"Excuse me." An attractive brunette squeezed by them to get to the napkins. She paused briefly and gave Mace a wide smile.

He smiled and nodded politely at the woman as he moved out of her way. "Good morning."

The woman looked at the wet spot on his shirt, then glanced at Zurie with an "ooh, girl, you didn't" smirk on her face.

Zurie stepped to the side with him, feeling like she wanted to disappear. But she needed to get over it and apologize for dumping coffee on him.

She set the half-empty plastic cup on the condiment station, dropped the soggy napkins in the trash and snatched dry ones from the dispenser. "I'm so sorry." She dabbed the wet spot on his shirt. "I can't believe I was so clumsy."

Mace took hold of her hand and the damp napkin. "It was an accident."

As the warmth of his fingers seeped into hers, Zurie's heart rate kicked up. But then she started free-falling into his gaze. Something that calmed and excited her all at once almost tempted her into leaning into him. "But I've ruined your shirt."

"I can wash it. I'm just glad it wasn't hot coffee."

His mouth curved upward into a wider smile that was even more intoxicating than his eyes.

Tall, hot... And her mind didn't need to go there. This was Mace—Tristan's good friend, whom she used to tutor when he was in high school.

She pulled her hand from his and stepped back. Droplets of coffee had landed on the front of his loose black athletic shorts and running shoes. She'd really made a mess of his clothes. "Now you're going to have to take everything off."

Mace's brows shot up. "Excuse me?"

"I meant, you'll have take off your clothes at home when you're alone…without me…because that's what you'll have to do to…you know…clean them."

What in the world had she just said, and did it sound as outrageous to him as it had to her?

His amused, puzzled expression answered the question.

"I need to go. Rina's waiting for me." Zurie headed for the exit.

Mace stood in line at Brewed Haven, ignoring the curious glances at his shirt, but the scents of coffee, chocolate and caramel wafting from him were harder to overlook.

The replay of Zurie bumping into him ran through his mind. *Well, damn.* That hadn't gone as expected. He'd just wanted to say hello to her. Actually, he'd wanted to confirm it was really Zurie. Seeing her away from Tillbridge and wearing casual clothes was unusual. She should wear jeans more often.

"Hi, Mace. The usual?"

He shifted his thoughts from how good Zurie had looked and focused on the upbeat twentysomething brunette behind the counter. "Please. Thanks, Darby. And can you give me one of whatever Zurie Tillbridge ordered?"

Fifteen minutes later he picked up his small coffee and Zurie's iced caramel mocha. After securing Zurie's coffee drink in a cardboard carrier, he left Brewed Haven.

As Mace stood at the curb of the sidewalk waiting for traffic to pass, he took a long sip from his cup. The small boost of caffeine would get him through his workout but not prevent him from getting sleep later on.

He'd planned on going to the gym near the sheriff's department after leaving work that morning, but a little over an hour ago, after his shift ended, Tristan had texted him, asking that he stop by Rina's place. After he met with her, he'd run a quick five miles in town, then drive home to get some sleep. But first he needed a clean shirt. Luckily, he had an extra one in his gym bag in his truck. Considering how the one he had on looked, Rina probably wouldn't mind him changing in her bathroom. And since Zurie had mentioned she was going to see Rina, hopefully he'd catch her there so he could give her the drink.

As he crossed the street, condensation glistened on the side of the plastic cup of iced coffee. With the swirls of whipped cream and stripes of caramel and chocolate packed under the domed lid, the drink could have passed for dessert. He'd never have guessed Zurie was a sugar fiend. Not that he spent that much time around her. But it hadn't always been that way.

Fifteen years ago, he'd been a starting sophomore quarterback more interested in chasing girls than passing his classes. When he'd started struggling in statistics, his attorney father had hired Zurie, who was a math whiz and in college, and issued an ultimatum—work with her as his tutor twice a week and get all his grades up or quit football.

At first, showing up at the Tillbridges' house to see Zurie instead of just hanging out with his friend Tristan had been embarrassing. But soon he'd looked forward to seeing her. She'd been easy to talk to, and she'd been patient with him and taught him how to study more efficiently. He'd finished that semester with a solid A average in every class. After she'd stopped tutoring him, they still had a good rapport. A little over twelve years ago, when he'd enlisted in the Marine Corps right after graduation, she'd been one of the last people to hug him goodbye before he'd left town.

Memories continue to roll in as Mace reached his red crew-cab truck and took his black gym bag from the back seat. Four years ago, when he'd returned to Bolan instead of staying in Nevada, where his family had relocated, he'd noticed a change in her. She'd lost the happy gleam from her deep coppery-brown eyes and didn't smile as readily anymore. The loss of her parents and Tristan's father, Jacob, along with the responsibilities of Tillbridge, had taken a toll on her. When he'd first gotten to town, he'd let her know that he was there if she needed anything, but she'd dismissed him.

He'd gotten the feeling she was seeing him as the teen he'd been instead of the man he'd become. That had disappointed him, but he'd accepted her decision. Since then, her interactions with him had been cordial but brief.

Hell, what she'd just said to him in the café was the first spontaneous sociable conversation they'd had in years. And it might not happen again, considering just how fast Zurie had rushed out of Brewed Haven.

Chapter Four

Upstairs in Rina's apartment, Zurie sat on the cream-colored couch, the only furniture in Rina's living room along with a wooden coffee table.

The sun shining through large tinted windows on the side wall gleamed on the clear packing tape strapped over the top and sides of stacked moving boxes.

Rina had purchased an older home just outside town about a month ago that needed some TLC. Now that the contractors were done, she was finally making the big move.

"It's mimosa time," Rina sang out as she walked through the archway on Zurie's left from the kitchen, carrying two tall glasses filled with the orange juice cocktail. "They're not as fancy as iced caramel mochas, but they're just as refreshing. It sucks that you spilled your drink on the way up here. Are you sure you don't want me to call downstairs and have Darby bring up another one?"

"No. This is good." Zurie accepted a glass from Rina.

The way her morning was going, a breakfast cocktail might help. They were meeting about Tristan and Chloe's wedding, so champagne was appropriate, and Rina's breakfast cocktails were legendary.

Bottoms up. Zurie took a long sip, and disappointment assaulted her taste buds. No alcohol? Rina never skipped putting alcohol in her cocktails, unless… Zurie took a good look at Rina. She hadn't gained weight, but she did have that glow about her. Maybe it wasn't just caused by Rina being in love.

Rina paused in taking a sip from her glass. "Something wrong with your drink?"

"No. It's good. But is there a reason you didn't put champagne in it?"

Rina followed Zurie's gaze to her flat tummy, and her mouth dropped open. "You think I'm pregnant? The only reason I used spritzer is because I took the champagne to the house. But a baby?" She laughed and shook her head. "Scott and I aren't there yet. We do want kids if we ever get married, but not right away."

An image came to Zurie's mind of Rina in the future, baking cookies with her young children and wiping the crumbs from their happy faces as they munched on the finished product. When the time came, Rina would be such a good mom. It felt like yesterday when Rina was a child and she was looking after her. But time moved on, and change came with it.

Pushing back nostalgia, Zurie took her phone from her purse sitting on the coffee table next to Rina's laptop. "I spent the weekend jotting down some notes about the ceremony and the reception."

Rina stalled her with a raised hand. "Hold that thought." She grabbed her laptop. "Tristan and Chloe want to FaceTime with us."

"I thought we weren't talking to them about the wedding until the end of the week?"

"We still are, but—"

The doorbell rang.

"I'll get it." Zurie set her phone and mimosa on the coffee table and stood. Hopefully, Tristan and Chloe weren't trying to micromanage the wedding. Yes, it was their ceremony and reception, but getting things done would become a lot harder if they were constantly checking in about the plans.

She opened the door.

"Hi." A small smile tipped up Mace's mouth. "I thought you might want this."

He held out a beverage carrier.

A frosty duplicate of the caramel mocha she'd spilled on him, her accomplice in crime that she'd abandoned downstairs, gleamed accusingly at Zurie in the sunlight. "You really shouldn't have."

Rina walked up beside her. "Hi, Mace. You made it. And you brought coffee."

His smile widened as he looked to Rina. "Now I feel bad. I should have brought you something, too. This is Zurie's."

Rina's gaze leveled on his stained shirt. "Oh, I see." She smiled at Zurie with a knowing look then turned back to Mace. "That's okay. Thanks for coming by on such short notice."

"Not a problem." Mace stepped forward.

Seconds passed before Zurie registered he wasn't just dropping off her iced coffee but coming inside. Like an awkward dance, he tried to come in then hesitated until she moved out of his way. She took the beverage carrier from him.

He walked inside and exchanged a quick peck on the cheek with Rina. "Do I have time to change before we talk?"

"Go ahead." Rina shut the front door and pointed down the entryway hall. "Bathroom's all yours."

"Thanks."

Once Mace was inside the bathroom, Zurie faced the humorous speculation in Rina's expression head-on. "Yes, that's my caramel mocha on his shirt. It was an accident. The end." She went through the archway on the left into the white marble–countered kitchen.

Rina followed. "It's kind of funny. You spilling coffee on Mace, and him bringing you another one. It reminds me of the day Scott ran into me." A sappy, distant expression came over Rina's face. "I was so mad at him for smashing my blueberry pies, but I forgave him, and look where we are now."

Exasperation fueled Zurie's eye roll. "I can't take it."

"Can't take what?"

Love. Tristan walked around with a perpetual grin, and Rina wasn't any better. Not everything was about love oozing happy vibes all over the place. Some things really were just a clumsy, unfortunate accident.

Zurie took the drink from the holder and stuck the cup in the refrigerator. "It's not the same as what happened with you and Scott. Spilling coffee on Mace was embarrassing. And to make it worse, I told him he should take his clothes off. What I really meant to say is that I'd gotten coffee on his shorts, too, and he was going to have to wash them along with his shirt."

"You told him that?" Rina laughed, but empathy shone in her eyes as she propped a hip against the counter. "I'm sure he didn't take it seriously, especially since you're not one of the women around town drooling over him. Last week, when he was at the café, from the looks a few of the women were giving him, they really were imagining him without his clothes. But last I heard, the owner of the doggy day spa snapped him up. Wait…no. They might have broken up. Darby saw him having dinner with the new personal trainer at the fitness center. But that was weeks ago, too. I wonder who he's dating now?"

"You're right. I'm sure what I said didn't faze him." Zurie waved her hand over the top of the automatic trash can and dropped the cardboard carrier inside it. And she wasn't fazed by Mace. So what if he fit the description of Lily's prescription? That didn't mean that Mace was the cure, ridiculous as it was.

Rina gave her a contemplative look. "Mace may not be your type, but there's a cameraman working on the movie set who's single. Scott knows him well."

"I'm not interested in dating anyone. Period. Why is Mace here?" Zurie lowered her voice. "Does he know about the wedding?"

Rina offered up a shrug as they walked from the kitchen through the archway leading to the living room. "I'm not sure what he knows. When you got up to answer the door, I got a text from Tristan about Mace stopping by and that we had to bump the call fifteen minutes."

Zurie settled near the end of the couch and picked up her mimosa.

Rina sat closer to the opposite end and picked up hers.

A short time later, Mace joined them. As he

dropped his bag on the floor near the wall, Zurie forced herself not to stare, but it was hard not to appreciate how the white T-shirt he'd changed into molded to his pecs or how his shorts showed off his muscular legs.

Rina held up her half-empty glass. "We're having virgin mimosas. Would you like one?"

"No, thanks, I'll pass." He bent down and adjusted the laces on one of his light gray tennis shoes. "You're all packed up."

"I wish." Rina quietly chuckled. "I still have to sort through stuff in the bedrooms."

"Are you planning to rent this place out?" he asked.

"Not as an apartment. I'm converting the living room into an extension of the kitchen and putting in commercial appliances. Once the café starts taking online orders, we'll need the extra ovens and equipment to keep up. And this—" Rina swept her hand in a gesture encompassing the room "—will become a small conference space that I'll rent out for events."

Mace nodded. "I can definitely see it."

Zurie sipped her drink. She could, too, but what about the cost? Six years ago, she'd been totally against Rina buying and sinking money into remodeling the freestanding older building that housed the café and apartment versus renting one of the newer storefronts. Like she'd predicted, the upkeep of the place was more expensive.

Hadn't there just been an issue with the upstairs plumbing? Upgrading the pipes for the commercial kitchen was going to be a huge expenditure. Sure, Rina would have more income from the online business, but that could take a while to really kick off. And what about Rina's personal reserves? Surely she'd taken a hit to her savings with the renovation of the house. Had Rina thought it all through? Concern made Zurie fidget in her seat. Maybe she should talk to Rina about it?

No. She shouldn't. Not acknowledging Rina's success as a businesswoman in her own right had been one of the things that almost ruined their relationship.

Rina checked the time on her phone. "Tristan should be calling soon." She scooted over to the end of the couch and patted the middle cushion between her and Zurie. "Move over, Zurie, so Mace can sit down and see the screen."

Zurie hesitated. It did make sense for her to shift to the middle of the couch instead of Mace crawling over her. She scooted toward Zurie.

Mace sat down. A good twelve inches separated them, but his body heat reached across the space. "Tristan didn't tell me why I needed to be here. Does it have something to do with the engagement or the stable?"

Zurie looked to Rina in silent communication. He

knew about the engagement. Should they tell him about the private ceremony?

From the look on Rina's face as she answered him, she understood Zurie's unspoken question, too. "Not sure."

As if on cue, Rina's phone and her laptop rang on the coffee table at the same time. Rina answered from her laptop.

Tristan's and Chloe's faces appeared on screen. He was in the driver's seat, and she was in the front passenger seat of a car. "Hey," Tristan and Chloe said in unison as Chloe gave a wave.

"Mace." Tristan gave a bro nod. "Thanks for taking the time for this. I really appreciate it."

"You said it was important." Mace moved closer to the middle of the couch. His arm grazed Zurie's, and tingles expanded across her skin.

He peered down at the screen. "Where are you two headed?"

"Nowhere." Chloe laughed. "We're sitting in the car because it's the only place where we can talk about the secret wedding ceremony."

Mace reared back a little. "Secret wedding ceremony? Since when?"

Tristan chuckled. "Since Zurie talked us into it. She's our wedding planner."

"She is?" Mace looked to Zurie.

Growing overly warm under his gaze, Zurie grabbed her phone from the coffee table and focused on opening her notes app. "You should probably bring Mace up to speed."

Tristan's expression sobered a little. "We're having a small private ceremony at Tillbridge in five weeks, but we're keeping the details a secret from the general public. If anyone asks what Zurie's up to, she's helping Chloe plan an early surprise party for my birthday. A party for me shouldn't be a big deal to anyone selling news to the tabloids, but once things start happening the day of the ceremony, and people figure out what's going on, word will spread. We need a security plan to screen out unwanted visitors. Chloe and I were hoping you could help us out."

Security plan. Zurie added it to her notes. She hadn't thought of that, and it hadn't been on the wedding planning checklists she'd looked at online. But this wasn't the usual wedding.

"Consider it done." Mace looked to Zurie. "We should get together soon to work through some details. Do you have time tomorrow night?"

"Well..." Out of habit, Zurie pulled up her schedule on her phone. Seeing blank spaces on her calendar hijacked air in her chest. No. It was supposed to be that way. Kayla had remotely cleared all her Tillbridge meetings and tasks and handed them off to Tristan. She definitely had time. "Yes. I'm free."

In her suite at the guesthouse at Tillbridge, Zurie sat on her new blue yoga mat in the living room, legs crossed, feet not quite tucked into lotus position, but close enough for her to practice the new breathing exercise she'd stumbled upon online while looking up wedding planning checklists. The one from the beginner's meditation video she'd found on YouTube wasn't cutting it. This one was the heavy-duty upgrade she needed to take her mind off work…and Mace.

They were having an early dinner at his place at four thirty that afternoon. It made sense for them to meet there instead of a public place to discuss the wedding, but…

Stop thinking about Mace. You're meditating, remember?

Zurie recalled the instructions from the article. She hadn't read through every paragraph, just the important parts.

Back straight. Hands resting lightly on the thighs. Third eye open. *Third eye. That was one of the chakras. What was it about?* Maybe she should stop and look it up. *No, you shouldn't. Just breathe! Long exhale for three seconds... Inhale for five...hold for...*

A light tingling started in her nose, and she sneezed.

Dust...

Wiping down the furniture, vacuuming and doing some general cleaning would help fill the time until she went to Mace's house for dinner. Would his personal trainer friend be there? Of course she wouldn't.

The wedding was a secret. It would just be her and Mace. Alone.

Stop! You're losing focus again. Come on, Zurie, you can do this. Clear. Your. Mind.

Zurie wiggled into a more comfortable position.

If only Lily hadn't mentioned a hot guy that day in her office, having dinner with Mace wouldn't be a big deal. She had to stop thinking of him that way... but when did Mace turn into Mr. Tall, Hot and Irresistible, anyway?

Her thoughts went back to yesterday morning at the café when she'd bumped into him. Instead of being upset, he'd smiled and held her hand...kind of. He'd just stopped her from trying to do the impossible—clean iced coffee from his shirt. Still, for a brief moment, she'd felt comforted and attracted to him. And that's why her mind had gone rogue and she'd told him, in public, to take off his clothes. What had she been thinking?

Ha! You know exactly what you were thinking about. Ugh! This is impossible. Zurie stretched her legs out and flopped back on the mat. She couldn't keep her thoughts off him for fifteen whole minutes. And he wasn't even in the room. How was she supposed to make it through dinner at his place?

Chapter Five

Mace checked the whole chicken roasting in the oven then stirred the pot of *arroz con gandules* on the stove. Bay leaves, oregano, *sofrito* and other fragrant seasonings wafted from the rice and pigeon peas.

Home.

That's what he thought of whenever he made this dish. It was one of the ultimate comfort foods that brought up memories of sitting around the dinner table with his older brother, Efraín, their younger sister, Andrea, and their parents.

No matter how busy his father had been working as an attorney in Bolan or the number of cases his mother had on her desk as a school social worker, making time for dinner as a family most days of the week had been a priority.

He hadn't fully understood family meals as a teen, but once he'd moved away from home and joined the military, and experienced scarfing down MREs during training and deployments and eating in crowded chow halls, he'd come to appreciate the significance of those intimate moments during his childhood. There was something special about sharing a meal with the people you loved.

A text buzzed on his phone on the beige counter. As he glanced at the screen, he smiled. Even miles away, it was as if his mom had a sixth sense about when family was on his mind.

As he set down the spoon and picked up his phone, pictures buzzed in of his mom, dad and his mom's older brother, Dariel, standing outside the house where his uncle lived in Bayamón, Puerto Rico.

Past hurricanes had impacted the power grid system in the city. His parents were helping Dariel with the installation of solar panels on the roof of the pale green house that he'd painstakingly rebuilt with their help after Hurricane Maria had devastated the island. Once they left his uncle, they planned to visit other family members in the area over the next month. Then they were headed to Florida to see Andrea and her husband and their newest grandchild.

A flurry of texts and emojis went back and forth between his mom, Andrea and Efraín, who were also part of the group text. Mace joined in, asking questions about how the install was progressing. His mom texted back that things were going well.

The doorbell rang.

She's early. But then, he wouldn't expect anything less from Zurie.

After sending a quick text promising to catch up with everyone later, he set down his phone and went to answer the door.

He opened it and the greeting on his lips died out, leaving him speechless.

An inner radiance brought out even more of the beauty in Zurie's face, and her white sundress with splashes of sunflowers highlighted her tantalizing curves and silky-smooth-looking skin.

Maybe he should have made more of an effort and put on something other than a black T-shirt and jeans.

Holding a square pastry box in her hand, Zurie gave him a polite smile, then her gaze shifted to her brown sandals while tucking her matching clutch tighter under her arm.

Remembering his manners, he opened the door wider and stepped out of the way. "Come in."

"Thank you." Zurie walked inside, and the tantalizing scents of lavender and vanilla trailed after her.

He shut the door.

"I forgot to ask if I should bring something, so I

took a chance and brought these." She held the box out to him. "Nothing fancy, just cookies."

"The cookies from Brewed Haven are great."

"Oh no, they're from Pasture Lane. I didn't think about bringing dessert until it was almost time for me to leave, so I just ran to the kitchen and Philippa packed these for me. But you're right. The cookies at Brewed Haven are special." A look of doubt crossed her face, as if debating if she should give the box to him.

He slipped it from her hand. "Philippa's cookies are just as good. Thank you."

"Don't let Rina here you say that, and please don't tell her that I brought them to you."

The genuine look of discomfort on her face surprised him. Did she really think he would tell someone? He gave her a reassuring smile. "It's our secret. But make sure to leave room for dessert after dinner. I'm not eating these cookies all by myself." He gestured to the living room. "Take a seat and relax. Can I bring you something to drink? I've got flavored sparkling water, soda, wine, beer."

"Wine sounds good."

"White or red?"

"Red, please." She set her purse down on the wood coffee table in front of the dove-gray couch. "Can I help with anything?"

He had dinner under control, but from the way she lifted and dropped her hands, she needed something to do with them. Mace pointed toward the kitchen. "Sure, follow me."

As they walked inside, Zurie sniffed the air. "It smells amazing in here. What are we having?"

He set the cookies on the counter. "Oh, nothing fancy." Mirroring what Zurie had said to him a few minutes ago earned him a small smile from her. "Roast chicken, *arroz con gandules* and salad."

"*Arroz con gandules.* I like that dish."

"When's the last time you had it?"

"In Florida, a couple of months ago. I was filling in as a visiting professor at a college near Tampa. A friend that lives down there took me to dinner at a Latin restaurant."

"How was it?"

"Good."

Mace took a bagged mixed green salad kit from the fridge. "The chicken will be done in about fifteen minutes. All that's left is making this and setting the table."

"I can handle making the salad."

"That's perfect."

Zurie washed her hands in the sink.

Her methodical movements had a graceful quality that kept him glancing over at her as he slipped a bottle of merlot from the small silver rack on the counter. She was so deliberate he could practically hear her counting off the right length of handwashing time in her head.

Thorough. He could respect that.

As he popped the cork on the wine, she picked up the bag of mixed salad greens he'd left next to a bowl and wooden salad paddles on the counter. "It says prewashed, but I'll give them a quick rinse, just in case."

"Let me get you a colander." Mace found what she needed in a lower cabinet and went back to the wine. He poured her a glass, then filled another wineglass with sparkling water.

He handed her the wine. "I'd join you, but I'm working tonight. "*Salud.*" He lifted his glass in a toast to their health.

She clinked her wineglass to his and took a small sip. "Mmm. This is good."

"It's from a vineyard outside town."

"The one near Tristan's house?"

"No. This one's farther out. If you haven't already, you might want to take a look at their wine selection for the reception. I have their brochure somewhere around here. I can find it for you, if you're interested."

"Thanks." Zurie rinsed the salad in the sink. "Using wine from a local vineyard would be a nice touch. Details. I'm learning that's what planning a wedding is all about."

Her jumping in to plan the wedding? That's the last thing he'd ever imagined happening. As far as he knew, Zurie hadn't missed a day working at Tillbridge in years. Not even when she'd sprained her ankle a while back. Tristan had been so frustrated with her because she wouldn't even let him help when her crutches got stuck in the mud near the stable.

Prickles dancing on the back of his neck, a sensation that he got when something wasn't quite right, started up. Curiosity almost prompted him to ask her lots of *why* questions.

But this was just dinner and helping her plan security for the wedding, not an interrogation.

He took plates down from an upper cabinet and silverware from a drawer. "So I guess you heard that I'm Tristan's best man?"

"Yes, but of course he chose you."

"You make it sound as if he didn't have other options. He could have chosen a friend from his bull-riding days. I'm honored he asked me."

"Rina and I feel the same way about Chloe. Unfortunately her friend that she wished could be there is on location shooting a film in Europe and can't attend the ceremony. She asked Rina to be her maid of honor, and I'm acting as an honorary one, since I have to remain free to coordinate the ceremony."

"How is the planning going?"

"Good." Zurie shook the salad in the colander over the sink, getting rid of the excess water before putting it in the bowl. "Rina is primarily responsible for the cake, but Philippa's going to help with decorating it, I think. And Philippa's also handling the food for the reception. They have a ton of ideas. I understand, it's Chloe and Tristan's day and they're excited for them, but we're going to have to pare things down to the best options. I can help them do that. Chloe and Tristan said they were okay with me choosing the menu, based on the things they said they liked, to save time, but I think we can loop them in with a family get-together at Tristan's or Rina's house. That way we can meet up without it being too suspicious."

The buzzer on the stove went off. He took the chicken out of the oven and set it on one of the unlit burners. "Sounds like a good way to get things done."

"I hope so. The other big thing aside from the ceremony details and security is Chloe's dress. She found this place that operates like one of those online personal shopping companies where they send you clothes to try on based on your preferences. But the try-on limit is three dresses. I'm afraid she'll just end up choosing one because she won't have time to send them back and get three more."

"That doesn't sound like a good option. And isn't the dress a big deal? When my sister tried on wedding dresses before she got married, she had my mom, her future mother-in-law and two of her close friends with her. From what I understand, it was a memorable bonding moment."

"That does sound really nice." Zurie mixed the

parmesan cheese and croutons into the lettuce. "But with all the secrecy surrounding Chloe and Tristan's plans, we can't go to a bridal place for her to try on dresses. Unfortunately, it's another thing she'll have to give up, along with not formally announcing the engagement or wearing her ring. I wish it didn't have to be this way for Chloe."

The sincerity in Zurie's face held his attention. She always came across as practical, but she really was disappointed that Chloe couldn't have more when it came to choosing a dress.

"Have you considered sneaking Chloe in under the radar to see Charlotte at Buttons & Lace, like early in the morning or late at night?"

Charlotte Henry and her dress shop, Buttons & Lace, had been a fixture in Bolan for at least a couple of decades.

"We could, but..." She held up the salad dressing packet. "Do you want me to hold off or mix it in?"

"Mixing it in is fine with me if that works for you. You could, but what?"

Zurie opened the packet and poured it in. "We're trying to keep the need-to-know list to a minimum. I'd have to loop Charlotte in on things."

Charlotte didn't socialize with the locals who liked to gossip. She also didn't seem the type to collaborate with the tabloids, but whether or not to trust her wasn't his call.

"What does your gut tell you about trusting her?"

Zurie used the paddles to mix up the salad. "I probably could. I mean, she was a good friend of my mom, and she'd probably love to help. But all it takes is one wrong person to be let in and the plan goes out the window. I need to be sure before recommending that we let anyone else in on what we're doing. What do you think?"

"I'm big on trusting my instincts. When I do, I'm usually right."

"Hmm." The slight curve of her lips came with her contemplative expression. "I'll think about it."

Mace slid carving utensils from the butcher block on the counter. His instincts were definitely telling him something about Zurie. Planning this wedding was important to her, but he couldn't shake the feeling that there was a lot more to it.

Chapter Six

Zurie sat at the table in the dining room adjacent to Mace's kitchen.

While they ate, he went over some basic details about security for the wedding. But her mind kept wandering.

It really should be a crime for him to look that good...

Natural waves traced through his black hair. The shadow of a beard on his cheeks and jawline framed his easy smile, and she couldn't help but stare as it gradually came into his eyes. His shirt and jeans fit as if they were tailor-made for him—snug but not too tight, giving tantalizing hints about the muscle underneath. The total package of Mace was all kinds of distracting.

"So in my opinion, we'll need a security team of at least seven or eight people." Mace picked up the wine bottle and gestured if he should top off her glass. "Most likely, they'll be a mix of the more trustworthy guards from the security company already working at Tillbridge and some acquaintances I know I can count on."

She really should say no to the wine, but it was so good, and she was feeling more relaxed than she had in ages. Zurie nodded yes to the wine. It was so easy to talk to him. The Mace she remembered had always been talkative, but in an immature way, as if he'd been trying to impress her. But the Mace sitting with her now was confident in himself and his words.

When he finished pouring, she took a sip, and the merlot's mellow warmth settled into her. "Isn't that a lot of guards for a small ceremony?"

"Not really. Between securing the perimeter of the property for the outdoor wedding, then monitoring what's going on at the guesthouse during the reception afterward, we'll need them. Tristan's right. Once people start realizing what's going on, they'll get curious. And we'll want to be ready for anything, since Chloe has started getting weird fan mail."

"What? She has a stalker?"

"From what Tristan told me, it's not at that level of concern. Just fans that are really excited for the upcoming movie. It's not unusual, just something that comes with Chloe growing more popular as an actor, along with the loss of her private life."

Zurie paused in lifting her glass. She really hadn't considered just how secretive this ceremony had to be. Or that maybe it might be more of a hardship for Tristan and Chloe to go through with it.

"Uh-oh." Mace interjected into her thoughts. "What's that look about?"

She set her glass down after taking a sip. "I'm starting to wonder if Rina and I made a mistake by pushing the issue of Tristan and Chloe having a ceremony here. I thought they were settling for less, but eloping might be less of a hassle for them."

"No. I agree, they *were* settling. At least, I know Tristan was. When he mentioned eloping to Vegas to me as an option, I could tell it wasn't what he really wanted. When he asked me to be his best man last night, he was really happy about the ceremony, and he said Chloe is, too. You planning this for them is a gift. They wouldn't have said yes if they didn't feel that way.

"I hope so. Otherwise I'm being selfish."

"Selfish? How?"

The story of her doctor's visit with Lily almost slipped out. The wine must have really gotten to her. She'd never considered confiding in Mace in the past. Not that she spent that much time around him. Or made him feel welcome.

Memories flitted in from four years ago, shortly after Tristan had left Tillbridge. Someone had vandalized signs on the back road, and Mace had come by in an official capacity to see if the staff or a guest had noticed anything unusual the night before. As he'd left her office, he'd told her to call him if she needed anything. A part of her couldn't wrap her mind around him no longer being the slightly cocky teen she used to know. And Mace had reminded her of Tristan. She'd made it very clear to Mace that she didn't need his help.

Remorse over the way she'd dismissed him that day stole her appetite, and she nudged her plate away. He'd either forgotten or he'd forgiven her. People forgiving her seemed to be the story of her life lately.

Mace waiting expectantly brought Zurie back to his question. As she searched for answers, one she hadn't thought of until that moment emerged. "I don't know. I guess I wanted to do it because Mom loved celebrating things. Not just national holidays or birthdays or us winning a rodeo event, but things like the last day of school or the first day of summer. And we always celebrated King Day and Juneteenth and, of course, the Tillbridge Spring Fling." Wonderful memories surfacing in her mind made her smile. "And then there were the really obscure holidays like national corn dog or national Popsicle day."

Mace smiled with her. "I remember being at your

house once on national Popsicle day. Your mom made some from fresh peaches."

He remembered that? "Yeah, she used to make all kinds, but the peach ones were her favorite."

"So Chloe and Tristan's wedding is a way of rekindling the way your family used to celebrate things?"

The absence of her mom, along with her father and uncle, hit Zurie, turning her memories bittersweet. "In a way, I guess it is."

Mace laid his hand on hers. The warmth from his touch reminded her of how he'd taken her hand when she'd tried to clean up his shirt at Brewed Haven. Just like then, his firm but gentle grasp felt calming. He let go, and she immediately felt the loss.

Suddenly, needing to do something, she arranged her silverware on her half-empty plate. "If you're going to make me eat cookies, I better start moving around. I'll do the dishes." Zurie stood, and lightheadedness assaulted her. As her vision swam, she reached for the edge of the table.

"Whoa, hey, I got you." Mace grabbed hold of her waist and guided her back down to the chair. "Feeling dizzy?"

"Yes."

"Put your head between your knees."

Zurie moved to lean over, but a faint pounding started in her head. "Bad idea." She sat back up, and cold prickles rained over her.

Mace hunkered down in front of her, concern creasing his brow. “I think you should lie down on the couch.”

Embarrassment aside, it did feel like she might topple out of the chair. “Okay.” Zurie stood. Mace kept an arm around her all the way across the room to the couch.

Once they got there, she sat down, slipped her feet out of her sandals and stretched out. “I just need to lie here a minute.”

“Can I get you anything?”

“Water, please.” She massaged her temples, which had started to ache. “And some aspirin?”

A moment later he returned with both.

His gaze remained on her as she sat up long enough to pop two pills in her mouth and chase them with water. Then she lay back down on the black-and-white throw pillow.

Mace put the glass she’d handed him on the coffee table along with the bottle of aspirin and sat next to them. “Are you feeling a little better?”

“Yes. I probably just got up too fast.”

“Maybe.” He studied her. “How much have you eaten today?”

It was confession time. “Probably not enough to compensate for a glass of wine.”

“Dizziness and headaches—has it happened before?”

"Dizziness, sometimes. Headaches, yes. More so lately."

"Have you been to the doctor?"

"I have." The genuine concern in his eyes pulled out more. "I saw Lily last week." Everyone knew about Lily and the family practice she'd assumed from her father a few years ago. "She said I'm stressed out. But I've been doing everything she told me to do—getting more rest, trying relaxation techniques, eliminating caffeine."

"Oh, I see." He crossed his arms over his chest. "So when I replaced your caramel mocha yesterday, I was aiding and abetting."

The humor in his tone prompted Zurie to give him a wistful smile. "Yes, you could say that. But I miss coffee so much. I hate giving it up."

"It's hard at first, but it'll get easier. You should give up alcohol, too, until you're past caffeine withdrawal. That's probably why you're having more headaches than usual, and in some people, it can cause dizziness, too."

Caffeine withdrawal? Great. How long would that go on? Defeat and a sudden wave of tiredness hit her at once, and she sank into the couch. "This whole destressing thing is harder than I thought it would be. I'm even failing at meditation, and that's just breathing."

"Does Tristan or Rina know about you needing to reduce your stress?"

"No. And you can't tell them. I don't want to take away from the excitement of the wedding."

"So your version of following your doctor's orders to relieve stress is planning a wedding all by yourself?"

A huffed laugh escaped, and her head protested with a small throb. "I'm on a staycation for the next three weeks. It's the only thing on my calendar. I can handle it."

"Let me help you."

"With what, the wedding? You already are."

"No. I mean not just with the security. Everything. I can even teach you a few relaxation techniques."

"Seriously?" She couldn't keep skepticism out of her tone.

"Is that so hard to believe?"

The Mace she remembered from years ago was a sports junkie and always on the move, never standing still. "I appreciate the offer, but it's not necessary." She went to get up, but he stopped her, placing his hand on her shoulder.

"It's necessary if you don't want me to tell Tristan and Rina that you almost passed out in my dining room. The only way I'm keeping what you told me a secret is if I'm watching out for you. Take it or leave it."

Mace looking after her? The prospect of that didn't sound relaxing at all. But from the look in his eyes, he wouldn't change his mind. Zurie lay back down. "I'll take it."

Mace stuck a detergent pod in the dishwasher and closed it. He'd turn it on later so he wouldn't wake up Zurie.

Earlier, after she'd reluctantly accepted his help and agreed they should postpone talking about the setup plan and security needs for the wedding until tomorrow morning, he'd returned to the kitchen to put away the leftovers and clean up. When he'd gone back to check on her, he'd found Zurie sound asleep.

Maybe he shouldn't have agreed to keep what was going on with her from Tristan. Stress wasn't anything to play with. It was a sign she wasn't taking care of herself. But this wasn't his story to tell. Again. The Tillbridges and their secrets…

A little over four years ago, Tristan had showed up on his doorstep looking as if his world had been ripped apart. And it had. A dumpster fire of lies involving Tristan was threatening to consume Tillbridge. The only way Tristan saw that he could stop that from happening was to leave town for a few years—or possibly decades. And not tell anyone why except Mace. After failing to talk Tristan out of the plan, he'd driven him to the airport in Baltimore the next day to catch a flight out of Maryland.

Tristan had put his family over his own needs. And now Zurie was doing the same.

Mace's phone rang on the counter. He snatched it up and glanced at the caller ID before answering the video call. It was his brother. "Hello."

"Hey." Efraín, a slightly older, leaner version of Mace with light brown hair, frowned at him on the screen. "Why are you whispering?"

"Hold on." Mace left the kitchen and walked down the hall away from the living room and into the first door on the left. "A friend is sleeping on my couch."

"A friend, huh? Is it the one who owns the pet store?"

"She owns a day spa for dogs, and no. It's not her."

Mace shook his head. His personal life always seemed to be up for discussion with his family. As a defense attorney and now head of the family law firm, Efraín was even more relentless than him at finding out answers. But there was nothing to tell. Sure, he'd met a few women for coffee or taken them to dinner, but as far as someone he wanted to spend quality time with—he hadn't found that connection with anyone yet.

But if he mentioned that Zurie Tillbridge was the one on his couch, that would lead to a full-on inquiry and interrogations from Efraín, Andrea and his father—all lawyers.

Their interest wasn't unwarranted. His friendship with Tristan, and Zurie tutoring him years ago, wasn't his family's only tie to The Tillbridges. When his father had practiced corporate law in Bolan, he'd provided legal advice to Mathew and Jacob Tillbridge on more than a few occasions.

Mace quietly shut the door and walked farther into his home office–slash–workout room. "Like I said, she's a friend. You didn't call to find out who I'm dating. What's up? Everything good with you, Gia and the kids?"

"We're all doing great. It's busy now that Gia is back to working full-time at the hospital and the kids are in pre-K. Things are also picking up at the firm."

Mace started filling in the next sentence in his head. The question his family had started asking him ever since he'd completed law school almost a year ago—"When are you taking the bar exam and moving to Nevada?"

The sound of a little girl's voice filtered in through the phone, Efraín glanced down and offscreen. "*Sí, es tú tío.*" Moments later, Efraín's four-year-old daughter, Emilia, sat on his lap staring at Mace from the screen.

A riot of honey-colored curls framed her adorable face. "*Bendición, Tío.*"

Hearing Emilia asking for his blessing of protection, something he, Efraín and Andrea had been taught to do as children to show respect to their elders, made him smile as he sat on the weight bench.

He responded. "*Que Dios te favorezca y te acompañe, princesa. ¿Como estas?*"

"*Bien.* Where are you, *Tío*?"

"I'm in Maryland. Where are you?"

"My house." Efraín whispered in her ear, and she continued, "When are you coming to visit us?"

"I'm not sure. Hopefully soon."

Bored with the conversation, she squirmed on her father's lap.

Efraín smiled down at her and pointed at the screen. "*Dale un beso.*"

Emilia placed her hand over her mouth, and when she took it away, she made a vibrating sound with her lips.

As Mace threw back the kiss, he did the same with his lips and she erupted into giggles. Before he could say, "Bye," she slipped out of her father's arms.

Efraín looked over his shoulder and called out in Spanish for her and her twin brother, Leo, to stop running in the house. He turned his attention back to Mace. "What happened with you coming to visit after you attended that training seminar in Sacramento? Was it canceled?"

Mace pulled up a mental calendar. He still planned to travel to California for the crisis-negotiation seminar. But now that Tristan's wedding was the week after that, and he'd just insisted Zurie let him help with the plans, he'd have to return right after he completed the training to continue assisting her.

But he'd already canceled a prior trip to Reno to see Efraín. Doing it a second time would probably seem like he was stalling on the plan of joining the law firm Efraín and his father had opened when they'd moved to Nevada seven years ago, Calderone and Associates. Especially if he told Efraín he hadn't been studying for the bar exam.

Tension gathering along Mace's shoulders prompted him to shrug it off. It wasn't the end of the world. The deadline to apply to take the bar in Nevada was about two months away. Once he applied and was accepted, he still had six months before taking it. Plenty of time to study and make plans to relocate to Nevada. He just needed to focus on helping Zurie with Tristan and Chloe's wedding first.

"I'm still attending the conference, but something else has come up. I have to return to Bolan earlier than expected."

Efraín's release of breath conveyed a lot. Now that their father had recently retired, Efraín wanted him there to firm up plans to join the firm sooner than later. "So I guess you'll let me know when your schedule frees up again?"

"I will.

Mace switched the conversation to the text they'd received earlier from their mom. Before the call ended, Mace also got a chance to see Leo and say hello to Gia.

Mace checked in on Zurie again. She was knocked out cold.

An hour later, he had showered, shaved, brushed his teeth and dressed in a casual long-sleeve black pullover, jeans and dark Lugz boots. If Zurie wasn't alert enough to drive, he could take her home. After dropping her off, he'd still have time to get to the department and change into his uniform before the start of his shift at nine.

In the living room, Zurie snuggled into the pillow and mumbled in her sleep.

From the smile on her face, she was having a really good dream. Too bad he had to wake her. Crashing on his couch for the night while he was at work was an option, but knowing her, she'd refuse.

Mace leaned down and shook her gently by the shoulder, but she didn't wake up. Not wanting to startle her, he spoke softly. "Hey, Zurie."

Blinking sleepily up at him, she laid her palm to his chest, and her warmth seeped into him. Her full lips parted with a sigh. "Mace…" Zurie raised her head, curved her hand to his nape and kissed him.

Chapter Seven

Zurie let herself fall into the dream. *This is wonderful...*

She held an iced caramel mocha, three times larger than the normal size. Just as she went to take a sip through the gigantic straw, Mace appeared out of nowhere and slipped the drink from her hands. That wasn't very nice of him. She really should be frustrated about that, but his mouth was suddenly more appealing than the iced coffee. In her dream, she gave in to temptation and pressed her lips to his.

As he murmured her name, the deep timbre of his voice spread like melting chocolate on her tongue. Desire stretched and expanded inside her as if it had just awakened after a long nap, refreshed and ready to go. Zurie dived into the kiss, reveling in the decadent warmth of his mouth.

Warmth? She shouldn't feel warmth in a dream.

Wakefulness fell like a line of dominoes, and she opened her eyes. *Oh no...*

As their lips separated, his gaze held questions. But the slight fullness of his lower lip and the faint taste of peppermint on hers answered her own. They'd kissed. Or, based on the bewildered expression on his face, she'd kissed him.

Mortification surged through her, and she sat up, causing him to move back.

"I'm sorry." She snatched up her nearby sandals on the floor and stuck her feet in them. "I'm..." No other words could fully encompass her dismay or embarrassment.

He dropped down next to her on the couch. "It's okay. It's no big deal."

Maybe it wasn't for Mace, but for her this was... She couldn't even look at him. Zurie sprang to her feet, rounded the coffee table and grabbed her purse. "I should go."

"Zurie, wait."

"Thanks for dinner." Her legs couldn't take her out the door fast enough.

Outside behind the steering wheel of her car, she backed out of the driveway. Her tires briefly squealed as she braked, then sped down the street in the middle-class neighborhood with near identical, neatly built houses and manicured lawns. As she reached the main road and navigated through nighttime traffic, she glanced in the rearview mirror. Mace hadn't followed her. A hint of disappointment mingled with relief.

A few stop lights later, she made a left turn and headed to Tillbridge. With miles ahead of her on the less populated, darkened, two-lane road, she set the cruise control and let her mind go back to the kiss.

She couldn't blame what had happened on Lily and the prescription. Yes, Mace checked all the boxes of tall, hot and irresistible, but she'd been the one who'd messed up and kissed him. What was her excuse? Caffeine withdrawal? *Ha!* Yeah, right. The urge to tongue tangle with one of the best-looking guys in town probably wasn't listed as a symptom. And neither was how, during those seconds of losing herself, not one single worry had entered her mind. She'd just wanted to keep kissing him. She hadn't felt that with anyone since…

Nope! Not going there. Dredging up a past relationship wouldn't help. Mace had said that it wasn't a big deal. Why should it be? He had a doggy day spa owner, a personal trainer and a long list of other people he'd dated in town. Kissing her had just been a tiny blip on his radar.

Zurie breathed past the weird disappointment settling in her chest. Once she got home, she'd drown it out along with her embarrassment in a god-awful cup of chamomile tea. And then, after a good night's sleep, she'd figure out what to say to him about it in the morning when he came by to talk about the wedding.

Mace halted his truck at the intersection at the end of the empty tree-lined road. To the left, the sheriff's department was less than fifteen minutes away. To the right, he was even closer to Tillbridge.

Usually he could compartmentalize things and control his thoughts, something he'd learned to do well as a marine. But tonight, not even the string of potholes on the back-road shortcut had shaken the memory of kissing Zurie. Sure, he'd told her the kiss was no big deal. But he'd wanted to kiss her again so badly, he'd had to sit down on the couch afterward and get his head straight.

When he'd first returned to Bolan a few years ago, he'd been interested in getting to know Zurie better. But with all she had going on with her family, and Tristan entrusting him with his secret before leaving town, asking her out hadn't been close to the right thing to do. Zurie shutting him down and refusing his help had made it even easier to let go of the possibility of ever dating her.

But that kiss she'd given him less than an hour ago… Maybe he'd just imagined the desire he'd felt from her. Had she really whispered his name? Or had

Zurie been half-asleep, dreaming of kissing some other guy, like the one in Florida who'd taken her to that restaurant?

Needing answers, Mace turned right.

As he drove down the smooth paved road, the smell of lush green trees and grass filled the cool night breeze coming in through the open driver's side window. The earthy smell of horses reached him just before he spotted the dark railed fence surrounding the acres of land owned by the Tillbridges.

Bypassing the turn that would have taken him along the pasture to the stable, he drove farther down to the twenty-room guesthouse. Since he'd taken the shortcut out of town, he'd probably beaten Zurie home.

He pulled into the full lot and drove past the two-story white building with a pitched roof.

A couple sitting in rocking chairs on the lighted porch in front of windows framed by green shutters looked out over the gently sloping grassy incline that flowed into a fenced-in pasture lit up by moonlight. The horses that grazed there during the day were either gathered in the run-in on the other side of the field or had been taken back to the stable. Night or day, the view was beautiful.

As he approached the far end of the parking lot, his headlights illuminated Zurie's Mercedes in her reserved space. She was just getting out of her car.

Mace backed in beside her, turned off the engine and got out of the truck.

Lights from the porch of the guesthouse helped lessen the shadows.

Surprise and something he couldn't place was on Zurie's face. "Mace, what are you doing here?"

"You forgot something."

"What?"

"An explanation for why you kissed me."

"Isn't it obvious?"

Not in the mood to guess or try to figure her out, he got straight to the point. "No. It isn't. You either liked kissing me or you didn't. Which is it?"

"Does it matter? You said it was no big deal." She gave a shrug of indifference, but the slight hitch in her voice indicated the opposite.

"I know I said that, but I was wrong." Mace stepped closer to Zurie. "You kissing me, it matters."

"That kiss. It can't happen again."

"If that's what you want."

She closed her eyes and shook her head. "Why did you have to follow me?"

Chances. He'd taken more than his share in his life. But answering her question was one of the biggest ones yet. "I liked kissing you. And I wanted you to know that."

Her long lashes raised from her cheeks, and what they revealed took his breath away. Before he could recover, she gripped his arms and sealed her mouth to his. As she parted her lips, he glided in, tasting the desire he'd witnessed a minute ago in her eyes. His heart went haywire.

Mace curved his hands to her waist, bringing her closer, and need hummed through his veins as he explored the curves and hollows of her mouth.

If only he had more time.

He eased back, breathing out at the same time she did as they let go of each other. He cleared his throat. "Glad we got that settled."

"Have we?" The appealing fullness of her lips, and the slightly stunned look on her face, almost pulled him right back in for another kiss.

"Yes. Or at least the important part is settled." The kiss at his house and the one they'd just shared weren't small occurrences they could just ignore. But as far as what to do about them… Mace backed away. "I need to get to work. We'll figure this out in the morning."

Chapter Eight

Zurie walked into her private suite of rooms on the second floor of the guesthouse and shut the door. As she leaned back against it, she touched her mouth, recalling the wonderful feel of Mace's lips on hers.

When he'd pulled up in the parking lot earlier, she'd gone through a mental inventory of her possessions, thinking she'd left something behind. Keys, phone, lip balm. She hadn't accounted for Mace's confession. Or kissing him again. But she'd needed to know if she really had enjoyed it or if she'd just been caught up in her dream. And now she had an answer—and no idea what came next.

Pushing away from the door, Zurie tossed her

purse on the navy couch and went to the adjoining bedroom. A nice long shower and a good night's sleep would help give her some perspective.

Later on, she sat under the crisp white sheets on her bed, leaning back against a pillow on the headboard. She drank a dreaded cup of chamomile tea, waiting for sleep to creep up and knock her out in the tranquil sanctuary she'd carefully cultivated with ash wood furnishings, a large white rug on the light wood floor and warm beige textured walls.

"I liked kissing you. And I wanted you to know that..."

Why hadn't Mace just left the first kiss at "no big deal"? Now that they both knew that they liked kissing each other—and, judging from that second kiss, they liked it a lot—what could they do with that? He said he wanted to talk to her, but it wasn't like they could take things further. No matter how easily those kisses took away her troubles.

But what about how she'd felt around Mace tonight when she hadn't been kissing him? Somewhere between prepping the salad and sitting at the dinner table, her anxiety had naturally lessened. Just like when she'd spilled coffee on him at the café and he held her hand. But it was ridiculous to think that he was some kind of sexy, magic chill pill. And even if he was, the relief would be temporary at best. Look at his dating history. And hers. While he dated around, she didn't go out often. And when she did, it was always when she was out of town. That way she didn't have to answer questions or put up with speculation about her personal life. And if she and Mace were to take things further, it could become a little too personal, since Mace and Tristan were friends.

So that settled it. The answer to getting involved with Mace was no…right?

At six in the morning, Zurie gave up on sleep and sat up in bed. If she tried again, she'd just fall into the same sensual dream of her and Mace that had plagued her whenever she had managed to drift off. But just as bad, the desire she'd felt in the dream still warmed inside her.

Mace would be at her door in a little over two hours. It was going to be impossible to look at him and not see those images. She needed them harnessed and under control before she and Mace talked about last night. Going over the wedding plans first, away from her suite, would give her the mental distance she needed before the "we kissed, now what" conversation.

She picked up her phone from the nightstand. Maybe Tristan would be able to meet her and Mace at the south pasture pavilion later that morning. The pavilion was where Tristan and Chloe wanted to say their vows. After meeting there, the three of them could take a quick drive around the property to discuss the security plan Mace had in mind to keep things in order during the ceremony and the reception at Pasture Lane. Having Tristan at the meeting with Mace would help prevent other distractions.

Zurie fired off a quick text to Tristan asking if he could meet them at eight. Less than a minute later, he responded that he could.

A small rush of relief went through her as she set the phone back down and got out of bed. Maybe her attempt at adding a new normal to her routine—meditating in the morning—would help as well.

After an hour of separating clothes to drop off at the dry cleaner's and completing a few loads of laundry, she was ready to give clearing her mind a chance. Zurie unrolled her blue yoga mat between the flat screen on the wall and the glass coffee table in front of the couch.

She got into position and closed her eyes.

Mace had said they'd talk in the morning. When he arrived in about a half hour, what was he going to say to her? What would she want to say to him? When she saw him, would every ripple of muscle underneath his clothing remind her of what she'd dreamed of last night?

Suddenly, her white tee and blue yoga pants felt warmer than a parka. She dropped her head in her hands. Was she feeling this way because she was in some sort of man drought? Or had those two kisses with Mace really changed how she felt about him?

A knock reverberated through the room.

Her heart bumped against her rib cage as if it were trying to leap out of her chest. Zurie rose to her feet. *You've got this.* She wasn't a teenage girl with a crush. She was a grown woman.

Zurie checked the peephole, then opened the door.

He stood in front of her, even sexier than her dreams.

As Mace stared, as if taking her all in, her expanding heartbeats took up space, not leaving her much room to breathe. "Hi."

"Good morning." He crossed the threshold into her space.

The appealing scents of sandalwood and citrus enveloped her. Every pore of her skin opened, welcoming the heat of his, and her resolve to distance herself from her attraction to him started dissipating into thin air.

A small smile tipped up his mouth, and in her periphery, she spotted the flexing of his bicep. As he started to reach for her, she stepped back, opening the door wider for him to walk in.

She caught the infinitesimal raise of his brow.

Accepting her silent invitation, he came inside. "Did you sleep well?"

As she turned from him to shut the door, denial sat on the tip of her tongue. No, she wasn't a teen with a crush, she was a grown woman who knew how to handle problems. Big ones. And she'd always dealt with them head-on...along with facing the facts.

She'd liked kissing him. What had avoiding her attraction to Mace done for her so far? Nothing but raise her anxiety level and rob her of sleep. Being near him did make her feel more relaxed. Maybe in some odd way, Lily's prescription was right on the nose. And staring right at her now.

Zurie faced him. "No. I didn't sleep well at all."

He frowned. "What kept you up?"

"You." Before she could second-guess herself, she let the whole truth out. "You caused it."

Mace studied Zurie a moment. He walked over to her, and the same inviting warmth she'd felt a minute ago when he'd gotten close moved over her like a slow, gentle caress.

His gaze held hers. "How can I fix it?"

In his face, Zurie saw what she was fighting—desire. But she was losing the battle.

"I'm not sure if that's a good idea." Still, a light-as-air sensation guided her forward onto uncertain ground. A place where there were so many unanswered questions. And possible consequences.

"If you want me to leave, I will."

"No. I don't want that."

His unwavering gaze held hers. "What do you want, Zurie?"

Anticipation and excitement, a long-buried heady mix she used to harness right before a barrel-racing event, surfaced. He curved his hands to her waist, and it rushed in even stronger. Her heart rate ticked up. For nearly seven years, she'd played it safe and not let herself get close to the edge like she had as a competitor—to go fast on her horse with all the trust in the world that she'd be able to control the outcome.

Running Tillbridge required steadfastness and practicality at all times. But right then, she wasn't in charge of running the stable. She didn't have to keep her actions or herself in check. She could do the one thing being the primary keeper of her family's legacy didn't allow her to do—just feel.

Hunger for just that had her lifting up on her toes as Mace leaned in. She met his mouth halfway. Relief and longing brought a moan out of her as she escaped into the drift and glide of an unhurried, deepening kiss. This is what she wanted—real, unadulterated passion and not just memories or a dream. She wanted him.

Mace picked her straight up, and she wrapped her legs around his waist. Having helped Tristan configure the alarm system in her apartment, he knew exactly where to go, but kisses that grew more urgent with need halted the journey every three or four steps.

He picked up the pace, and in a few short steps, they reached her bedroom. As soon as he set her feet on the floor, their clothing became a minor obstacle they raced to take off each other. The final reveal was him sliding down his briefs.

Desire uncoiled inside Zurie.

Mace glided his hands around her bare waist and brought her flush against him. From breast to hip, she melded to his deeply muscled torso. His sweeping, openmouthed kisses down the side of her throat mesmerized her, and the grip of his fingers along her hips made her heart speed up. Mace molded his hands to her butt, pressing his hardness to her lower belly, and her legs became weak.

He backed her up to the bed and followed her down to the mattress. As he explored every inch of her, she eagerly arched up for his kisses and caresses. Her palms traveled over him, meeting rippling muscle under heated skin.

Mace paused to roll on the condom he'd tossed on the bedside table, then guided himself inside her. The outside world faded and narrowed to just that moment. Soon, her shaky breaths became moans as strokes and glides grazed over needy places, awakening more want.

Joined with him, moving with him, she stared into his whiskey-colored eyes, falling deeper into desire.

Pleasure built. Tantalizing her. Teasing her. It drew out cries of *yes* that she couldn't contain and left her hovering on the precipice before she dropped into ecstasy…more wonderful than any stretch of her imagination.

Chapter Nine

Zurie lay in Mace's arms, tucked into his side. Her hand on his chest rose and fell with his slow, even breaths as he slept.

Contentment and the embers of desire ready to spark again—they drifted inside her. Along with something unexpected. Peacefulness. Mace radiated it in his sleep. Usually, she couldn't stand to lie around this late in the day, but right there next to him, she just wanted to stay snuggled to his side.

Her phone buzzed with a text on the bedside table. Careful not to wake Mace, she slipped from his embrace, picked it up and glanced at the screen.

I'm running behind. Can we meet at 8:30 instead?

Crap! She'd forgotten about meeting Tristan.

Mace, still asleep on his back, turned his cheek to the pillow. He needed to rest. And when he woke up, they needed to talk.

Something came up. Can we try again tomorrow?

Dots floated across the screen as Tristan responded.

Even better. Will 8:15 work?

Relief pushed out a breath.

Yes.

Good. Tell Mace I'm sorry. Packed schedule.

Will do.

Tristan gave her reply a thumbs-up emoji.

A small seed of guilt started growing larger as she lay on the bed. What if Tristan had asked her what had come up? Would she have lied to him?

Zurie glanced at Mace. They had to get a handle on things before the situation got too far out of control.

* * *

Mace walked out of the bathroom, fresh from the shower, tightening a blue towel around his waist.

In front of him, the bed was empty.

Where did Zurie go? A small bit of unease pinged in his gut. He snagged his jeans from the side chair, where she'd laid them, and put them on.

He'd awakened at around noon, slightly disoriented and surprised to find Zurie asleep in his arms. Happiness had quickly followed along with the realization he needed to rethink his game plan. He'd left her sleeping and hopped in the shower to get his thoughts in order.

On the drive over to Zurie's place that morning, he'd worked through the various scenarios of what would happen when he arrived. One, she'd immediately want to hit the reset button and forget what happened last night. Two, she'd admit she felt something when they'd kissed, but hesitancy would keep her from wanting to move forward. Three, they'd be on the same page about spending time together.

The curveball she'd thrown him when he'd walked in a few hours ago had been entirely unexpected, but not unwelcome. Zurie wasn't easy to read, but if he guessed, the two of them sleeping together didn't automatically default to option three.

Where was his shirt?

A quick glance around the room didn't reveal its whereabouts.

In his bare feet, he walked out into the living room.

Zurie sat on the couch with her legs curled under her, scrolling through info on her computer tablet, wearing his black pullover shirt. It fit her like a loose dress, draping over her knees. She'd rolled the sleeves up to her wrists.

Her feeling comfortable enough to wear his shirt was a good sign, wasn't it?

She glanced up and then looked back down again. Her dark hair hid her face. "We'll have to postpone going to the pavilion and walking the property until tomorrow."

He went over to the couch, but she still didn't look at him. "Why? What's up?"

She swiped her finger across the screen. "I asked Tristan to join us this morning, but he couldn't make it, and now a rainstorm is coming in."

Mace caught her hand in midswipe. "I'm sure we can find other ways to occupy our time. Like talking about what happened this morning."

As he gently tugged Zurie to her feet, he slipped the computer tablet from her hand and laid it on the glass coffee table. The scent of soap wafted from her. She must have showered in the other bathroom. But afterward, she'd still preferred to put on his shirt. He couldn't stop a pleased smile.

"Mace, I'm..." She lifted her other hand as if to lay it on his chest but stopped short. "I'm not sorry about what just happened between us this morning. But I shouldn't have allowed it to get in the way of what we were supposed to be doing. Tristan and Chloe's wedding should have been the priority."

He caught her hand before she dropped it and brought it to his chest with his. "Yes, Tristan and Chloe's wedding is the priority, but we're still going to get the things we need done. I don't see any reason why we can't balance planning the wedding and being together."

Being together... There, he'd said it. The ball was in her court now.

A long moment passed.

Zurie flattened her hand against him, and the heat of her palm on his skin brought up memories of her soft caresses earlier. His heart rate picked up. "If we were to keep seeing each other, we couldn't tell anyone, not even Tristan, Rina or Chloe. My personal life has never been a factor at Tillbridge, and I wouldn't want it to become one now."

Mace rested both hands on her waist. Not telling Tristan could go either way for him in the consequences department. But Tristan knew the type of person he was and that he'd never hurt Zurie. He'd always treat her with respect. But this wasn't about Tristan. This was about Zurie preferring to keep her personal life private. That was a legitimate ask.

"If you don't want to tell anyone we're seeing each

other, we don't have to. If that changes, it's because we made that decision together."

Zurie's brow furrowed slightly.

Uh-oh. Something else was on her mind. He gave her a slight squeeze. "What's bothering you? Tell me."

"Well—" Zurie sighed. She lifted her other hand to his chest. Her absently stroking over his pecs raised goose bumps. "While I'm off from work for the next three weeks planning Tristan and Chloe's wedding, I can do things out of the norm like sleep until noon or indulge in having fun. But once I'm back to managing the day-to-day here at Tillbridge, that has to be my sole focus."

Was she saying she couldn't manage Tillbridge *and* enjoy life? Mace studied her resolute expression and saw traces of how he'd been years ago.

He'd balanced undergrad studies and the marines, then law school and working as a deputy as his main priorities. He'd been the hamster on the wheel, living off spoonfuls of sleep and massive cups of coffee to survive. When he'd graduated law school and had time to sleep, work out, date, just hang out with friends or do things he liked, he'd realized how much of life he'd missed.

Enjoying the good moments was important to him now. Zurie being stressed out enough for Lily to advise she take time off was a sign she needed to learn to do a lot more of the same. It wasn't about eliminating fun and relaxation but finding a balance between the two. He could help her see how necessary that was while he helped her plan the wedding…and maybe they could continue to see each other afterward. He wasn't heading to Nevada for a few more months.

Mace widened his stance and brought her closer. "Okay. So it sounds like we have a lot to fit in over the next five weeks or so. Plan Tristan and Chloe's wedding. Teach you how to relax. Enjoy spending time together."

She shook her head. "We have three weeks."

"But the wedding is in five." Giving in to curiosity, he leaned in, searching out the scents of lavender and vanilla on the side of her neck.

"Yes, but three is when…" Sighing softly, she tilted her head, giving him better access as he swept kisses near her earlobe. "Mace, you're not listening to me."

"I'm listening, but maybe we should consider an even number, like five weeks. It's easier for me to remember."

Her hands paused in inching up toward his shoulders. "Five isn't an even number."

"Damn. After all these years, I still have problems with math." Mace covered Zurie's mouth with his, kissing away further objections.

Chapter Ten

Zurie drove the golf cart down the narrow paved trail bisecting the north pasture, headed to the stable to meet Tristan. Once she swung by and picked him up, they'd head to the south pasture pavilion to catch up with Mace at eight fifteen.

On one side of her, horses grazed in the pasture. On the other side, vans and trailers belonging to the movie production crew were parked near the indoor horse arena. The large sandstone-colored structure had been built to accommodate the needs of the filming, but the building was also something Tristan had wanted for years.

And he'd been right about the advantages. They

could bring in more income by conducting riding clinics in the indoor arena and offering it as a practice space for local competitors who participated in events like dressage and show jumping or other rodeo events. Or at least they could once the filming stopped.

The golf cart shuddered as it went over a cracked paver. That was the second one she'd encountered so far. She'd better remind Tristan to send the groundskeepers out to make repairs. Eventually, the jagged edges would rise. The last thing they needed was for a guest to trip and fall.

She reached the end of the paved trail that intersected with a wide gravel path. To the right, in the circular, fenced-in outdoor arena, one of the staff was giving riding lessons. The man and woman were riding Tillbridge-owned horses. Most likely they were visitors from the guesthouse.

Out of habit, Zurie took a long pause before she turned left. Satisfied there weren't any oncoming horses being ridden or led down the path, she took her foot off the brake, eased down on the accelerator and headed toward the stable.

As she approached, Tristan and one of the grooms walked out of the open double doors of the sandstone-colored building with a navy roof and trim.

She parked the cart on the side in the narrow graveled space outside the adjoining paddock on the left and waited for Tristan to join her.

But Tristan walked to the driver's side of the cart instead of getting in the passenger seat. Mild irritation was in his eyes.

Zurie picked up her phone from the cup holder between the seat and turned off the reminder alarm for their meeting that had started to chime. "Everything okay?"

"It could be better." He adjusted his navy ball cap with the Tillbridge logo—a white horse and *T* with a lasso. "We ordered pavers to replace the cracked ones on the path leading from the guesthouse to the stable. But the home improvement center delivered the wrong ones. Apparently, our order went someplace else. And they're all out of the ones we need for at least three weeks."

He had noticed the pavers. Good. "Did you try that company we used before in Virginia?"

"You're on a staycation, remember? I got this." Tristan glanced around, making sure they were alone. "Chloe purposely let it slip that you and Mace are helping her plan my early surprise birthday party. And with our meeting today, I told a few key people that Mace and I are reevaluating security protocols on the property because of the movie."

That made sense. A private security company currently monitored the property, including the movie set and base camp—the area where trailers for housing and production were set up for the cast and crew—in the west pasture, but Mace was the unofficial liaison between the security at Tillbridge and the sheriff's department. He was also Tillbridge's go-to consultant on security concerns at the stable.

"You mentioned you and Mace. What's my excuse for being here today?"

A small smile tipped up Tristan's mouth. "I told them that you can't stay away from business, despite being on vacation."

Yes, that *was* probably believable, considering her track record.

He took his phone from his back jeans pocket and checked the screen. "You up for a ride to the pavilion? We've got time. Thunder needs some exercise, and I'm sure Belle wouldn't mind tagging along. We can let them graze in the pasture near the pavilion while we check out the rest of the property. Mace won't mind stowing our saddles in the back of his truck while we ride around."

She quelled the urge to continue the conversation about suppliers for the pavers. "Sure. Let's do it."

A short time later, they were on the trail riding in companionable silence as birds chirped around them. Morning sun beamed through openings in the trees, warming her through her pale blue button-down and jeans.

Belle, a chestnut bay who fit her name, walked regally next to Tristan's ebony-colored horse.

Zurie settled into the Western-style saddle. The gentle ruffling of Belle's dark mane in the breeze, along with the sway of Belle's ears in front of her along with her rhythmic gait, were all like a soothing balm.

It was just as calming as the vibrational healing meditation app Mace had downloaded to her phone yesterday before he'd gone home for a power nap and to change clothes for work.

It was one of the relaxation techniques he used to help him sleep when he got home in the morning after work. He'd been right. The music along with the hypnotic voice guiding her through a relaxing visualization actually *had* helped her drift off to sleep.

Zurie shifted her thoughts from Mace. "Other than the paver issue, is everything else all right?" She caught the pointed but indulgent look Tristan gave her. "I'm not prying, just making general conversation."

"Yeah, other than the pavers, the only thing giving me a headache is Anna Ashford practically demanding that I make time for her to come to the stable so she can interview me. Just because she's got political connections in Bolan doesn't give her the right to demand anything."

The mayor's sister-in-law, also known as Annoying Anna, was in charge of the town's online newspaper, the *Bolan Town Talk*. The weekly paper was more like a blog filled with gossip and speculation than informative details about current events.

A piece of news that wasn't on her calendar or

the notes she'd passed on to Tristan before her stay-cation dropped into Zurie's thoughts. "Actually, she does. Remember that side conversation I mentioned having with the mayor at the business mixer about using his influence to change the order of construction for the main and back roads?"

"No." He groaned. "Tell me you didn't make that trade with him?"

"What choice did I have? It was either the interview with Anna or face the consequences of the construction schedule. She just wants the scoop on our future plans for the indoor horse arena once the filming of the movie is over."

"The pothole-infested road would have been easier to deal with. And you've been had. Last I heard, she was still bent out of shape about the mayor visiting the set of *Shadow Valley* without her when the filming started. The mayor made that trade with you because it was the only way he could free himself from her. This interview is a fishing expedition. Anna is either interested in digging up news about me and Chloe and the supposed love triangle with Nash Moreland or what's happening on the movie set."

Zurie huffed a chuckle. "Now who's dealing in gossip? If you're too afraid of her..."

Tristan gave a derisive snort. "I can handle Anna. But once I'm done fielding questions about me and Chloe and why I'm not taking her to the movie set,

I'll probably need a happy hour staycation at the Montecito Steakhouse bar. Let's change the subject. How *are* things going with your staycation? Other than planning the wedding, and not worrying about the stable, what else have you been doing to occupy your time?"

A memory of being with Mace for most of yesterday flashed in, and a mixture of butterflies and heat loosed inside her. "Oh, nothing much."

Were her hands actually getting sweaty? If she couldn't talk about Mace without getting flustered, what would happen when she saw him in less than fifteen minutes?

Sensing Zurie's anxiety, Belle lifted her head and shortened her stride.

As Belle started to lose the easy swing in her gait, Zurie automatically relaxed her shoulders and loosened up her hips, telegraphing to Belle that as her rider, she was still confident and in control.

Tristan glanced at Belle then Zurie. "You okay over there?"

"We're good." Zurie pointed to the gate just up ahead. "Let's go through this one instead of the one farther up. Belle could use a good gallop through the pasture."

"Sounds good to me."

At the gate, they both dismounted.

She managed the horses while he keyed the code into the locking mechanism and opened the gate.

After she led Thunder and Belle into the pasture, he locked the gate and they both got back on their horses.

Mischief filled Tristan's eyes. "Last one to the end of the field buys lunch." Without waiting for a response, he and Thunder started galloping across the pasture.

No, he didn't... Zurie turned Belle. When they were younger, he always used to pull this stunt. She gave Belle her lead, heading after them, and soon Belle's speed merged with the flow of her effortless gallop. As the sky and the empty green field flew past, the same focused rush she used to experience while maneuvering her horse around barrels in the rodeo ring at top speed came over her.

Soon Belle was only half a horse length behind Thunder and gaining fast.

They reached the fence separating the grass in front of the pavilion from the south pasture at the same time. Tristan slowed Thunder down to a trot, and Zurie did the same with Belle.

He grinned at her. "You almost beat me. Not bad for a desk jockey."

"Desk jockey? Look who's talking?" Zurie laughed. "You had an early start, and I still caught up with you."

"Yeah, I guess that is pretty impressive."

They brought their horses to a halt and dismounted. As they secured Belle and Thunder to the hitching post near the covered structure used for parties and special outdoor events, Mace drove his truck through the gate yards away from the opposite end of the pavilion and parked on the grass a distance from the horses and got out.

As he walked toward them, tucking his keys into the front pocket of his jeans, the ends of his casual beige button-down fluttered in the wind.

Zurie shifted her attention to taking her phone from a small holster attached to the saddle. How did she and Mace usually greet each other? A handshake. A nod. Why couldn't she remember?

Mace joined them. He and Tristan shook hands and came in for a brief thump on the back.

Mace gave her a nod and a friendly smile. "Hey, Zurie."

"Hi, Mace."

Now she remembered. Polite hellos were their usual. No friendly pecks on the cheek like he'd exchanged with Rina at the apartment above the café the other morning. If she recalled correctly, even Chloe received a peck on the cheek from him.

Disappointment pushed a quiet exhale out of Zurie. Because that wasn't her usual with Mace, they couldn't start now, especially in front of Tristan. But having a reason to touch him would have been nice. She'd have to wait until they saw each other after touring the grounds with Tristan.

"Does that not work for you?" Tristan stared at her.

Crap. What had she missed? "Why do you ask?"

He chuckled. "You're frowning like you hate Mace's idea."

"No, not at all." Zurie looked from Tristan to Mace. "I'm sorry. I zoned out. Would you mind repeating that last part?" If she'd missed more than that, Mace could fill her in on it later.

"Sure." Mace pointed toward the gate where he'd come in. "We can't let the guests park outside the gate like they usually would when they come here for events."

That left only one alternative. "Then everyone will have to park at the guesthouse and we'll have to transport them here."

"Exactly." Mace nodded. "That way we have total control over who's at the ceremony. Do you know the number of guests yet?"

Zurie flipped to the notes on her phone with the tentative guest list Chloe and Tristan had emailed her. "Twenty to twenty-five for the ceremony and fifty at the reception."

"Have you decided how you want to set things up here?"

"Our best option is a full tent. That's the only way to keep things hidden from view, especially during the setup. A bride's side, groom's side configuration out in the open would just be too much of a tip-off."

"Yeah, probably so." Tristan glanced around with a crestfallen expression. "But one of the reasons Chloe liked the idea of having the ceremony out here was the view. I proposed to her up the hill. She can't see it if we're in a tent."

"There may be a way around that," Mace interjected. "Why not set up the chairs for the guests under a couple of tents, but open the sides during the ceremony? You, Chloe and the minister can stand near the edge of the pavilion to take your vows."

Zurie tried to picture what he said. "But won't the tents still obstruct the view?"

"Depends on how you set them up." Mace gestured for her and Tristan to follow him to the edge of the pavilion.

They all faced forward. Tristan stood on one side of her and Mace on the other.

Mace turned partially toward her as he pointed. "If the tents are positioned on each side at a diagonal, Tristan and Chloe will be able to see the view of the pasture and the hill behind it. And with the front and side of the tents rolled up, the guests can see Chloe walk down the aisle and her and Tristan take their vows."

Zurie clutched her phone in her hand, fighting the urge to lean into where she'd fit so comfortably against his chest yesterday.

She took a step forward, putting space between them. "That could work. The main idea is to not tip anyone off before the wedding. Since the setup plan is supposedly for Tristan's birthday party, we'll label them on the diagram as tents for the buffet tables that we'll never set up. On the day of, it won't take long for us to arrange the chairs instead. So let's talk this through. The guests arrive at the guesthouse, believing Tristan's birthday party is at Pasture Lane, but we'll tell them there's been a change of venue, and we shuttle them out here."

"And then what happens next?" Mace asked.

Images started forming in her mind. "They arrive, someone makes the announcement that it's actually Tristan and Chloe's wedding, and we open the tents. Everyone sits down. Tristan, I think you should already be here with Mace. Chloe should be driven in as soon as everyone's settled. She arrives, walks down the aisle. Wait, back that up. Chloe walks down with her father to Tristan and the minister waiting at the edge of the pavilion." She looked back at Tristan. "You two exchange I dos, and then..."

From the happy look on his face, Tristan could see it, too. He and Chloe finally together as husband and wife. His phone rang, and he checked the screen. "I have to take this. Hold on a sec."

As he stepped away to talk, Mace walked next to Zurie. He leaned in and whispered, "Do you know how hard it is for me not to kiss you right now?"

She kept her eyes straight ahead. So he wasn't

immune. Goose bumps raised on her skin. "I guess you'll have to show me later."

"Yeah, but a lot later than I'd like to. I was tapped to cover an earlier shift. And I'm doing the same tomorrow. When we're done here, I have to head home and get some sleep."

Zurie's happiness deflated. She looked at him. "I understand."

The wind blew hair in her eyes.

Mace raised his hand as if to smooth it back for her, but then lowered it back to his side.

Tristan joined them. "I have to get back to the office. You two are going to have to finish without me. You can catch me up later."

Mace dug his keys from his pocket. "Actually, I was just telling Zurie, I can't go over the security plan today. I've been called in to work early."

Tristan clapped Mace on the back before turning away. "Thanks for coming out."

"No problem." Mace looked to Zurie. The longing she saw in his eyes made her heart swell. "I'll call you."

Chapter Eleven

Late in the afternoon at her place, Zurie sat on the couch checking items from her list on her computer tablet. Order the tents, chairs, portable wood runner—done. Close the guesthouse to reservations the day of the ceremony to just friends of Tristan and Chloe coming to Tristan's fake party—done. Schedule a private party at Pasture Lane for a fake customer to cover for the reception—she could check that off, too. Have fake invitations printed—still narrowing down the best place. Meet with Rina and Philippa to narrow down a menu—on the schedule. Dresses—that had to be taken care of soon.

What Mace had said about trying on dresses

being special had stayed on her mind. Tristan and Chloe's wedding was unconventional in a lot of ways, but finding a way to give Chloe this moment could mean a lot to her—finding the perfect dress, feeling good as she walked down the aisle, no regrets as she looked at her wedding photos years from now because she would see herself in a dress she really wanted. Maybe it was possible.

Zurie mulled over in her mind how her mom had looked forward to those rare free afternoons when she would catch up with Charlotte for lunch. Her mother hadn't been the gossipy type. She'd also valued loyalty and expected the same in return. If Charlotte hadn't shared those qualities, her mom wouldn't have counted her as a trustworthy friend. At least that's what her instincts told her about Charlotte and her mom's relationship. Maybe she should follow her gut instincts like Mace had suggested. Something she tended not to do.

Relaxing mental barriers, she confronted the close to seven-year-old mistake that had been hovering in her mind ever since she'd kissed Mace.

Theo Asher had been part of a group of fund managers from an investment firm in New York visiting Tillbridge. The CEO of the firm had paid Tillbridge a ridiculous amount of money for his people to experience working at the stable for a day.

Her father had given her the task of supervising the group as they mucked stalls, cleaned gear in the tack room, fed the horses, unloaded deliveries and helped with repairs. Some were able to jump right into the work, but Theo had been a disaster at manual labor. The areas he'd been assigned to clean were even messier than when he'd started, and he'd managed to break things no one ever had before. She'd been so frustrated with him, but when a horse had gotten spooked, he'd done the dumbest, bravest thing and jumped in to help. She later found out he'd done it to impress her and hidden that he'd hurt his wrist in the process.

Before Theo had left at the end of the day, he'd asked her out. Instead of basing her answer on reality, she'd acted on impulse and let her inner compass take the reins.

But this situation with Mace wasn't the same. She wasn't diving into a whirlwind romance, naively filled with unrealistic expectations. She wasn't ignoring the most important question—"where is this going?" With her and Mace, there were clear-cut boundaries and no expectations. She knew exactly when and how their situation would end in three weeks.

Mace had tried to get her to agree to staying together until Tristan and Chloe's wedding, but what she had with him fit in the same category of her staycation—a diversion that would come to an end as soon as she went back to work. But until then, she'd indulge.

Her phone rang on the coffee table, and she picked it up. *Mace*. Happiness perked up inside her. As she answered, she tucked her feet up under her on the couch. "Hello."

"Hey. How's your day going?"

"Good. I made a dent in the wedding checklist."

"Sorry I couldn't hang around today."

Zurie settled back on the couch and set her tablet aside. "It's not your fault that your schedule changed. Did you get some sleep?

"Yeah, I got a good six hours."

"Is that enough?" Lily had said she should try to get at least seven to eight hours every night.

"I've survived on less, and I'm powering up with some coffee. Oops. Pretend you didn't hear that."

Zurie's mouth watered. "I'm so jealous."

"I know your pain. I was downing too much caffeine once upon a time, but trust me. And trust Lily. Cutting back will be worth it."

"Seeing you, without the cup of coffee, would help." Oh, that sounded so cheesy. Zurie winced. She was really out of practice with flirting.

He chuckled. "It would, huh? What are you doing this weekend?"

"I'm helping Philippa and Rina pare down food and cake options for Tristan and Chloe to pick from. What about you?"

"I'm off this weekend."

"Well, since you insist on looking after me, I guess you're tagging along for the food tastings."

"Do you want me to tag along?"

What did she want? Answering that question as truthfully as she had yesterday morning—she shouldn't get too used to that indulgence.

"Zurie, it's a simple question. If you don't want me to go with you, just say so. I won't be offended. Looking out for you doesn't include me crowding your space."

"I want you there." As she said it, happiness rippled inside her. But maybe that sounded a little too desperate? "I could use a guy's perspective with the food, and you're perfect since you know Tristan well. Ten thirty at Pasture Lane tomorrow and eleven at Rina's apartment on Sunday. Can you make it?"

"Yes, I can be there for both."

"Good. And tomorrow, after the tasting's over, we could drive around the property and go over the security plan."

"That works for me. And Zurie?"

"Yes?"

"I can't wait to see you, too."

Chapter Twelve

Zurie checked herself out in the tall gold-framed mirror leaning against the wall in her bedroom. The casual, above-the-knee, sleeveless orange-and-white dress was bold and bright. Was it too much?

The dress with the sunflowers she'd worn to Mace's house had also been a departure from the navy, white, black and gray ensembles she usually wore. The simple color palette made it easier for her to mix and match outfits and get ready quickly for work early in the morning. But now she could explore the clothes in the back of her closet that rarely saw the light of day.

Dressing up a bit for dinner with Mace at his

house the other night had seemed appropriate. But today, was she making too much of things? They were just tasting food at Pasture Lane then driving around the property to talk about security. Maybe a casual top and jeans were more suitable.

"I can't wait to see you, too..."

The happiness that had come over her when he'd said it long hours ago made her twice as giddy now. But if that's how he felt about seeing her, shouldn't she wear something that made it worth the wait?

Downstairs, Zurie got off the elevator. The skirt of the orange-and-white dress swished lightly as she walked down a short blue-carpeted hallway.

Ahead of her, in the lobby boasting modern country-living accents, a few guests stood in line at the front desk.

Two smiling young women, crisp and efficient-looking in navy Tillbridge-logoed blouses, staffed the desk.

Zurie turned right and walked past a grouping of side chairs near a wall with gold-framed paintings of horses grazing in lush green fields near mountains.

When she reached the corridor behind the front desk, out of habit, she almost bypassed the glass double-door entry to Pasture Lane, heading for her office. It was so strange not being at her desk every day.

She'd been so tempted to work on the diagrams she'd created for the ceremony at the pavilion on the wide-screen computer in her office, but if she'd done that, she would have also given in to checking her business email. Right now, Kayla was screening her correspondence and only forwarding the ones Tristan couldn't answer to her personal email.

Using her computer or even going inside for something as simple as a paper clip or her favorite pen that was in the drawer of her desk was out of the question. But so far, quitting her office had been much easier than giving up coffee.

Inside the restaurant, she smiled at the young blonde woman in a crisp navy button-down and black slacks standing behind the podium. If Zurie remembered correctly, she'd recently been promoted to working at the host station.

Without glancing at her name tag, Zurie recalled her name. "Hi, Bethany."

Bethany smiled widely. "Good morning, Ms. Tillbridge."

"Am I at my usual table?"

"Yes. It's all set up for you."

Bethany moved to escort Zurie inside, but she politely waved her off. "No. You can stay here. I'm fine. Thank you."

The space with light wood tables and lime-green padded chairs was half-full. Most of the patrons sat next to a wall of glass overlooking the lush scenery that lay beyond a narrow wood deck. At ten thirty, it was the calm before the crowd that would steadily trickle in closer to noon.

Zurie set her phone on the four-top corner table tucked in the back of the dining room and sat down.

Two water glasses and two black coffee mugs were on the table, along with a carafe of coffee and a pitcher of ice water.

She automatically reached for the carafe but steered her hand toward the pitcher of ice water instead and filled up a glass.

Across the restaurant, Philippa, a tall woman in her late twenties, emerged from the kitchen through the faux-wood, double swinging doors. The lime-green bandanna securing her dark locks matched her chef's coat and the Crocs visible under the hem of her green-and-black-patterned pants.

As she drew closer to the table, Philippa smiled. "Good morning, Zurie." A faint southern lilt accented her words.

Zurie smiled back. "Good morning."

As Philippa moved to sit down, she hesitated, glancing at Zurie's empty coffee cup and full water glass. Her smile morphed into a concerned frown. "Is the coffee not brewed right? I'm sorry. The repairman who came into fix the machine this morning must have missed something. It wasn't just the water valve. I'd better go tell the servers to—"

"No, wait, Philippa. If you didn't get any complaints about the coffee at breakfast, I'm sure it's fine. I'm just not drinking coffee."

"You're not?" Philippa sat down and blinked back at her with an expression of disbelief.

Zurie conjured up her best "I'm okay" smile and sipped water. She really was okay. And no, the slight tremor in her hand wasn't because she was fantasizing about grabbing the carafe, ripping off the lid and guzzling down the coffee inside it.

Out of the corner of her eye, she glimpsed Mace walking in. Zurie took another sip of ice water, soothing her suddenly dry throat.

As he got closer to the table, he gave them a slightly lopsided smile. "Sorry I'm late." He sat in the chair to the right of Zurie and set his phone on the table.

"Hi, Mace." Philippa gave Zurie a quizzical look. "You're right on time. I think?"

Oh, that's right. She hadn't told Philippa that Mace was coming. "Mace is here to provide a male viewpoint on the food for...the party."

"Ah, got it, the party." Philippa smiled knowingly and nodded. "I'm serving you myself. That way you can tell me directly which items you want on the menu."

As Philippa walked away to get the food, Zurie turned her attention to Mace. He smelled of all things good. His slightly damp hair brought out its natural waves. A small, thin cut stood out on his angled jawline. Had he cut himself shaving?

He reached for the coffee carafe, nudged it away and poured water instead.

The teasing comment on her lips about his shaving skills stalled as she glimpsed a line of long cuts trailing up his hand from the back of his wrist. "You're hurt."

As he set the pitcher down, he glanced at his hand. "I'm okay." Mace gave her a tight smile, hints of weariness and something else appearing in his eyes.

"What happened?"

Mace's gaze slid over the room in a casual yet deliberate way then came back to her face. He lowered his tone for only her to hear. "There was a bad accident involving two cars on the main road leading to the interstate early this morning. Another deputy and I had to pry open the door to get to the young woman driving the car."

For a fleeting moment, Zurie's mind went to her mom, who'd lost her life in a car crash, and Rina, who'd almost died in one. Those moments were two of the worst days of her life. Her stomach dropped. "Is she okay? What about the other driver?"

"He's okay." Mace sat back in the chair. "But the young woman was airlifted to the hospital."

She couldn't completely understand how he felt about what happened, but it clearly weighed on his mind. "If you don't want to be here now, I understand."

"I could use the distraction. But I also don't want to bring down the mood, either. This menu is for a happy occasion."

"No. You're not bringing down anything." She almost reached over and laid her hand on his arm. "If it helps you to be here, stay. And if you need to talk, I'm here to listen."

"Thanks. I appreciate that, but I'm good." He gave her a small smile then glanced across the room to the kitchen doors. Philippa held a folded tray stand in one hand while expertly balancing a tray with plates on her shoulder. "Looks like the first course is up."

Zurie folded her hands in her lap. He didn't seem to be good. If only she knew what else to say to him. But if not talking about it any more was better for Mace, she'd leave it alone.

Philippa unfolded the stand and set up the tray. "We're starting with the appetizers. Anyone not eat anything or have allergies?"

Mace and Zurie both shook their heads.

"Good." Philippa gave them both small plates and silverware rolled in cloth napkins. "Let's get started."

Bite-size and mini portions of appetizers, based on foods Tristan and Chloe had said they liked, came and went from the table.

A little over a half hour later, Zurie and Mace had made their top choices, and Philippa had left them to finish the even harder task of narrowing them down while she plated up entrée selections.

Mace pointed. “The mini chicken sliders, nacho scoops and vegetable kebabs definitely get my vote.”

Zurie dabbed a white napkin to her lips. “They were good. I also liked the gazpacho soup in a shot glass, the shrimp cocktail shooters and the mac and cheese bites. The spinach balls were good, but I wouldn’t want to risk people walking around with spinach in their teeth.”

“True. What about the mini tacos and the grilled cheese?”

“I’d choose the mac and cheese bites over the grilled cheese. Less crumbs to worry about. The tacos are kind of similar in taste to the nacho scoops.”

“And less messy.” He pointed between two plates. “Pretzels or loaded waffle fry cones?”

“Not sure. What do you think?”

Mace munched on one of the mini cones. “Definitely these.” He chuckled. “They remind me of a particular dart game Chloe and Tristan played.”

“A dart game. What does that have to do with waffle fry cones?”

He beckoned her closer. “More than you think…”

Mace whispered to her about a dart game at the Montecito Steakhouse bar between him and Tristan against Chloe and one of the grooms who worked at the stable. A plate of loaded fries had been ordered during the game where things had gotten interesting between Tristan and Chloe.

As he relayed the story of the moment he believed had brought Tristan and Chloe together, he cracked his first genuine smile since he'd walked into Pasture Lane. Soon she was fighting to contain her laughter over what he described.

Philippa came back with a server who cleared away what remained of the appetizers and helped serve small portions of the entrée selections. Philippa sat down and chatted with them as they narrowed things down to apricot chicken, her famed smoked prime rib and spring vegetable pasta—a much easier task than with the appetizers.

"So I think we're good." Philippa tapped notes about all their selections into her phone. "Now we just need to set up a time for the final tasting." The one where Tristan and Chloe would approve the menu for the reception.

Zurie and Mace said their goodbyes to Philippa. Near the entrance, they slipped past the small crowd perusing menus while waiting near the host station to be seated.

They reached the corridor and headed toward the front desk.

He looked over at her. "You up for a short walk before we drive around the property?"

"Definitely. Actually, we could walk to the stable,

grab a golf cart and use it to ride around instead of using one of our cars."

"Sounds good to me."

Outside, a few guests enjoying the view and the mild afternoon mingled on the porch and walked the paved trail where they were headed.

When they were partway down the path dividing the north pasture, Mace's phone rang.

He slipped it from his front pocket. His expression sobered as he glanced at the screen. "I should take this."

"Go ahead." Zurie walked farther down the path, giving him privacy.

Her gaze gravitated toward where she'd noticed one of cracked pavers the other day. She couldn't find it. The delivery issue had been solved and it had already been repaired, thanks to Tristan.

Her gaze strayed back to Mace.

He rubbed the back of his neck as he stared at the ground, listening to whoever was on the line.

Anxiety rose inside her for him. Was it bad news?

Chapter Thirteen

Mace ended the call and caught up with Zurie.

He waited for her questions, but she didn't say a word, just started walking with him.

Mulling over how to break the silence, he tapped his phone to his thigh. "That was the deputy who was with me this morning at the accident. His wife is a nurse at the hospital where the young woman was airlifted. She made it through surgery. It looks like she's in the clear."

Zurie paused. "That's wonderful news." Smiling widely, she laid her hand on his arm.

On a reflex, he put his hand over Zurie's, needing just a few more seconds of contact with her as he allowed himself to fully absorb the good news. The helplessness and frustration that had balled inside his chest long before sunrise that morning began to dissolve.

He did his best not to carry the job home. He couldn't if he wanted to function. But when he'd gotten the car door open and looked into the young woman's scared but trusting eyes, he'd seen a grown-up version of little Emilia.

A breath escaped him along with the rest of the invisible weight he'd been carrying. "It's great news. Peyton's going to be okay."

As people walked around them, he dropped his hand from Zurie's, and she took hers away as they stepped to the side of the trail.

"Peyton? That's her name?" Zurie said. "What happened to her? What caused the accident?"

Realizing he'd said the young woman's name jarred him.

Normally he avoided talking about his job, even with his own family. Some things were hard to explain to anyone who wasn't a first responder. And because of his time in the marines and being a deputy, some people assumed his feelings chip had been removed. Yes, there were deputies who chose to wall off compassion, leading them down the dangerous road of not seeing people as people. But that wasn't him.

Mace looked down at Zurie's upturned face. He'd

opened up this conversation by mentioning Peyton's name, and his mood at Pasture Lane during the tasting probably did warrant more of an explanation.

"Yes, Peyton, that's her name. The other driver had been texting and driving and swerved into the wrong lane."

Zurie shook her head. "I don't understand why people think messing around with their phone while they're driving is a safe thing to do."

"At three in the morning, that road is mostly empty, so he probably thought he could take the risk. Luckily for Peyton, after the accident, he was able to call 911."

Mace recalled the scene when he'd first arrived. The nineteen-year-old-boy, bleeding from a head wound and feeling shaky, had still been in his SUV that was in the right-hand lane but facing the wrong direction. From the tire marks, Peyton's small two-door had spun out before flipping over on the side of the road.

Focusing back on Zurie, Mace continued. "She was conscious when the other deputy and I arrived, but she was wedged in. We couldn't get her out without possibly making her injuries worse. For some reason, she grabbed onto my hand instead of the other deputy's and held on. I stayed with her until fire and rescue arrived and got her out of the car and into the helicopter."

After they had airlifted Peyton out, he'd done his

job at the scene, but for the longest time, it was as if he could still feel her smaller hand in his.

Zurie reached down and clasped the same hand Peyton had held firmly in hers. "You say you don't know why Peyton reached for you instead of the other deputy. I do." As Zurie tightened her grasp, hints of soft emotions filled her eyes. "She knew you wouldn't let go."

Mace locked his truck parked at the curb on Main Street. Tucking his keys in his front jeans pocket and carrying his phone in his hand, he walked down the sidewalk toward Brewed Haven.

A couple of spaces behind him was Zurie's car.

After they'd ridden around the property yesterday, they'd spent time at his place, where he'd let her know how beautiful she looked and how much he'd appreciated her listening to him about the accident. And not saying the two responses he dreaded the most—"I'm sure she'll be okay" or "I'm sure you did the best you could."

When people said things like that, it always led him to change the subject. What could he say? Thank you? But with Zurie, he hadn't experienced that awkwardness, just understanding.

He was trying to give her the same when it came to them seeing each other, but sometimes it was hard. He'd been able to convince her that instead of settling for just a few hours at the stable, they could have more time together at his place. Unlike the neighborhoods in Bolan where many of the locals had lived for years, the newer subdivision he lived in consisted of recent transplants—couples by themselves or with younger kids. They were too busy living their own lives to notice or care how long her car was parked in his driveway.

Finally, they'd been able to really relax as they'd discussed wedding plans. Afterward they talked in between her devouring her new binge watch, *Star Trek Discovery*. It had surprised him how she'd become mesmerized with the sci-fi series.

He'd almost talked her into spending the night to keep watching it, but around nine, she'd insisted on driving home. She'd claimed that walking through the Tillbridge guesthouse lobby in the wee hours of the morning to get to her suite would have kicked up too much curiosity.

Mace crossed Main Street using the brick path winding through town square.

Days and nights were slipping by without them spending quality time together or having the opportunity to really know each other. Their undercover relationship was starting to play out like a tasting menu, where he could only have small bites, but he wanted the whole dating package with Zurie. He wanted to be able to hold her hand and kiss her whenever he wanted to in public, to take her on a date somewhere without her worrying if someone would see them. He wanted to see her let loose. Color outside the lines of what she deemed acceptable and live a little. But expectation ruled her choices. Could he ever get her to see past that? Did they have enough time?

Bypassing the entrance to the café, he jogged up the stairs to Rina's apartment and knocked.

The door opened, and Zurie stood in the threshold. A light breeze ruffled the skirt of her casual magenta dress, and her hair hung loosely around her bare shoulders.

"Wow." He gravitated inside, standing in front of her. "You look beautiful."

"Thank you." She looked up at him, and her smile made him want to stay right there, taking it in.

If he was going to get her to color outside the lines, this was as good a time than any.

Mace leaned in, holding her gaze, willing her to stay still and just let it happen.

The clang of what sounded like metal utensils landing on tile made him look down the hallway and caused Zurie to jump back.

So much for saying good morning to each other properly.

"Shoot!" Rina's voice came from the kitchen.

Zurie shut the door. "Rina's a little moody this morning since she was up baking for the half the night. I hope you didn't eat a big breakfast."

A few steps down the hall, as he glanced into

the kitchen on the left, he saw what Zurie meant. More than a half dozen decorated eight-inch round cakes sat on the counter. The way he was eating this weekend, he'd have to put in a workout every day next week.

Rina, dressed for work at the café and wearing a yellow apron, looked up from where she was sweeping coconut flakes from the floor into a dustpan. "Hey there."

"Do you need help?" Zurie stood beside him.

"No, I'm good." Rina dumped the flakes into the trash. "Take a seat in the living room. I'll be ready in a minute."

In the living room, the packed boxes, sofa and coffee table were gone, replaced by a lone six-foot table with a white tablecloth surrounded by four foldable chairs. Several forks, napkins, a stack of small plates and two empty glasses were in the center of the table, along with a small photo album with pictures of cakes.

The sound of utensils rattling in a drawer came through the archway up ahead on the left.

Mace set his phone on the table. As he held out one of the chairs for Zurie, and she sat down, he took his chances and pressed a kiss low on her neck.

Zurie turned her head to look at him and whispered, "What are you doing?"

"Saying good morning. You really do look beautiful."

"Good morning and thank you. Now will you please sit down and behave?" She looked more pleased than exasperated.

He grinned. "No promises, but I'll try."

"I'm ready." Rina carried in a cake from the kitchen, along with a small serrated spatula, and set both on the table. "Let's start with the basics. Vanilla cake with vanilla cream frosting topped with raspberries."

She gave details about the cake's ingredients and pointed out pictures in the album of how it might look as a tiered wedding cake. Then she cut a thin slice, cut it in half, and put the halves on two small plates before giving them to Mace and Zurie.

While Rina went to get water to cleanse their palates between tastings, they sampled the cake.

Sweet vanilla woke up his taste buds. "This is good." He sampled another generous bite.

Zurie sat down her fork. "It's definitely a possibility, but it might be a little too simple."

"What? Too simple?" he teased in a low voice. "I thought you didn't like complicated?"

"It's not that I don't like complicated. I just don't always have time to deal with it. But when I do, complicated is very...tempting. Like now." She glanced over at him.

Was she talking about cakes or something else? He leaned toward her. "Just how tempting *is* complicated right now?"

"Very tempting."

Her lashes dropped and raised as her gaze moved over him. When she looked into his eyes, his heart rate ticked up and almost obliterated his promise to behave.

And from her coy smile, she knew the effect she was having on him.

"Okay." Rina came from the kitchen carrying a pitcher of ice water and another cake. "Next up is red velvet with passion fruit filling and cream cheese icing."

Although she was known for her pies, Rina's cakes were equally delicious. But five cakes later, Mace suffered from a tiny bit of sugar fatigue.

Rina stacked saucers with the remains of cake, then picked up the half-full pitcher of ice water.

"Need a hand?" Zurie asked.

"No, I got it," Rina replied. "You two relax." Carrying plates and the pitcher, she went to the kitchen.

Mace sipped water. "How many more to go after this one?"

"Just two. I think." Zurie sank back in the chair. "Cake tasting is hard work. After this, I don't think I'll want to see another cake for weeks."

Rina came back in carrying the full pitcher and a white frosted cake dusted with coconut and topped with curls of dark chocolate. "This one's a little different. It's..." A ringtone like a doorbell sounded from the phone in the pocket of her apron. "Hold on." She answered the call. "Hey, Darby. Oh?" Her brows raised. "How many are broken? Yeah, that's a problem. Hold on. I'm coming down."

Rina ended the call. "I have to run downstairs for a minute. Zurie, can you take care of cutting this one? I won't be long."

"Sure." As Zurie picked up the cake cutter, Rina hurried out of the apartment. "I hope everything's all right."

"She said she won't be long, so maybe it's not serious."

Zurie hacked at the cake, cutting into it with less finesse than Rina.

He winced. During Tristan and Chloe's reception, she definitely needed to be kept away from helping to serve the wedding cake.

Mace resisted grabbing the spatula from her and motioned with his hands. "You might want to use the serrated side of the spatula, then slide it under to..."

She wiggled the spatula against the side of the slice and dragged it out.

"Or you could do it that way."

The small, mangled slice of the white cake with pale yellow filling barely made it to the plate before toppling over in a heap. "I'll take that one." She licked her thumb.

Her low moan of pleasure raised the hairs on his arms. "It's that good?"

"Oh my gosh, you have to taste this. It's part

cheesecake." Zurie snagged a clean fork, cut a bite from the messy slice and held it out to him.

He ate it, and the rich flavors of sweet coconut, tart lemon and hint of bitterness from the dark chocolate made him a release his own moan of contentment.

Zurie grabbed another fork, and they both gobbled up the slice.

As they licked their forks, their eyes met.

Before he could reach for the spatula, Zurie grabbed it and lopped off a much bigger, messier slice than the first. "Plate."

"Got it." His mouth watered as he caught the slice on a small plate and shoved another one under the second slice she dragged out.

They sorted out the slices and dived in.

"This is beyond good," Zurie said between bites.

He paused long enough to answer. "I don't know what she put in this, but she needs to patent it."

"She should."

A short moment later, Mace cleaned crumbs from his plate with this fork.

Zurie dropped hers on the empty plate and sat back in the chair. "I feel like I just had the most amazing out-of-body experience."

He could relate. Her leading the way to devour almost half a cake was totally unexpected.

Her gaze landed on the decimated dessert. "Rina isn't going to be happy about that. Once we were done with the tasting, I think she planned on selling the cakes downstairs."

"I'm sure she'll forgive us." His gaze was drawn to frosting clinging to the corner of her mouth. "You've got cake on your face."

She turned to him. "I do? Where?"

He picked up a napkin. Hell, she'd already gone way past the boundaries of expectation. Why not see what he could get away with?

Mace tipped up her chin with his finger and kissed the frosting away. "There got it. Wait. No, there's a bit more over here." He pressed his lips to hers. Instead of protests, her mouth grew pliant under his, inviting him in for a longer kiss that served up desire. Cupping her cheek, he went in for more, deepening the kiss.

The apartment door opened, and they broke apart.

Rina breezed into the room. Her gaze landed on the table, and her mouth dropped open. "What happened to my cake?"

Zurie's cute wide-eyed guilty expression made him snicker.

She shot him a look, but her lips twitched, and then Zurie did he last thing he ever expected. She snorted a laugh.

Chapter Fourteen

Zurie strolled out of Buttons & Lace dress shop on Main Street with a smile on her face, carrying a boutique shopping bag. She'd had a productive Tuesday morning meeting with Charlotte about wedding and bridesmaid dresses, and she'd even found a dress even prettier than the blue-and-green paisley one she had on.

She'd talked to Tristan yesterday about letting Charlotte in on the secret wedding and the possibility of doing something special for Chloe to find the right dress. Tristan had agreed, wanting the best and more for Chloe.

As anticipated, Charlotte had been excited to help.

She could even handle altering the suits Tristan had picked out for himself, Mace and Chloe's brother, Thad, who was now an honorary groomsman. But Charlotte also had a few ideas for alternatives that she thought Tristan might want to consider.

After Chloe's father and Thad mentioned going on a fishing trip instead of attending Tristan's "surprise birthday party," Chloe had let her family in on the plans for the ceremony. Aside from Chloe's family and Charlotte, Tristan had also told the stable's office administrator, Gloria. As a longtime employee at Tillbridge, Gloria had also been a trusted confidante and friend of Zurie's parents and Uncle Jacob. She'd volunteered to lend a hand with anything that was needed before or the day of the ceremony.

Blake, one of the trusted trainers at the stable, who, on occasion, filled in as driver for the guesthouse van, had been approached to assist with transportation the day of the wedding. He was organized, dependable and like a vault when it came to keeping matters confidential. On the day of the ceremony, with Blake corralling the guests and getting them to the ceremony, she could focus on synchronizing Tristan's and Chloe's separate arrivals at the south pasture.

Zurie neared the wine bar and shop. Contacting the sommelier at the shop to set up a time to sample wine and champagne for the reception dinner and toasts to the bride and groom was on her to-do list.

It was ten thirty. The business opened at eleven. Instead of calling, maybe she should wait around and make an appointment in person. After that, she'd stop by the florist. Then she had to get home and find out why the invitations for Tristan's "surprise birthday party" hadn't come in yet.

She crossed the street to the brick sidewalk surrounding the town square, where a sprinkling of pedestrians strolled through the grassy area with park benches and a fountain in the center of it. Walking to one of the benches nearest the fountain, Zurie took a seat and set her bag and purse beside her.

More cars and a tourist bus that hadn't been there when she'd gone into the dress shop over an hour ago filled parking spaces along the curb.

The casually dressed window shoppers were easily identifiable as tourists, while the locals gravitated like magnets in and out of the establishments lining the street. The rest remained engrossed in phone calls or sending text messages.

While she waited, maybe she could call Mace? He'd just been off that past weekend, so that meant, based on his two-two-three rotation schedule, he'd just come off work that morning and would go in again that night. So he was sleeping.

She missed him. They hadn't seen each other since getting in trouble with Rina over the cake. As Zurie thought about the moment, a smile crept up her mouth. Once they'd stopped laughing long enough to explain how good the cake was, Rina had tasted it herself. It was her first time making the coconut cake–lemon cheesecake combo, and even she had admitted she'd nailed it.

It had also inspired Rina to recall a nice memory. Whenever their mom had made lemon–poppy seed muffins, she'd have to hide them from Tristan and his father, because they shared a love of lemony desserts. But Tristan and Uncle Jacob were the perfect tag team, always managing to follow the clues of the lemon juicer on the drying rack, a bit of lemon rind in the sink or the discovery of lemon glaze tucked in the back of the refrigerator.

Like the loaded waffle fries, Rina's lemon coconut cheesecake creation appeared to be the perfect choice because of a personal connection to Tristan or Chloe.

"Aside from sitting there looking gorgeous, what do you do for a living?"

The familiar deep voice behind her, and what had to be one of the lamest pickup lines she'd ever heard, nurtured a smile. "Please tell me that line hasn't worked for you."

"You didn't like it? I've got a better one."

"I can't wait to hear it."

Mace rounded the bench and dropped down on the other side of her purse and bag. Based on his blue athletic shorts and gray shirt and his phone tucked in the pocket of a band wrapped around his arm, he was ready for a run.

He leaned. “Are you a parking ticket? ’Cause you’ve got *fine* written all over you.”

“What? Seriously? That’s the best you got?” She waved him off. But as *fine* as Mace looked in his running gear, that one may have worked for him.

He raised his brow in mock surprise. “Oh, you wanted my *best* line. Are you sure you can handle it? Because it just might make you want to crawl over here and kiss me.”

She didn’t need a pickup line for that. “I’m sure. Go for it.” Zurie schooled her features to neutral.

“Okay. I tried to warn you.” He leaned in and looked into her eyes. “Have you been covered in bees recently?”

“Bees? Uh, no, I hope not. Why?”

“Because you look sweeter than honey.”

“Sweeter than…” Laughter bubbled out of her. “That one was even worse.”

“How about, if you were a phaser on *Star Trek*, you’d be set to stun.”

She actually was stunned by how bad that one was. “Stop. You’re done. I can’t take it.”

“Wow. That really hurts.”

“I’m just trying to save you from future embarrassment.”

He sat back on the bench and grinned.

"Shouldn't you be in bed, resting up for work instead of practicing horrible pickup lines?"

"I should." His smile dimmed a little. "But I couldn't sleep."

"Oh no. Did something else happen at work?"

"No. Nothing like that. I'm good." He gave her a small smile and looked straight ahead for a moment and glanced back at her. "How did things go with Charlotte this morning?"

I'm good. That's what he'd said on Saturday before the tasting, and he'd given her that same small smile, but something had been wrong.

Pushing aside concern, Zurie went with the topic switch. "Really good. She's confident she can find the exact wedding dresses Chloe had planned to try on with the online dress service. And Charlotte is picking out a few other styles for Chloe to try on, just in case."

"You mentioned sneaking Chloe into the shop one night. Is that still the plan?"

"No. This morning Charlotte and I came up with a better one, pretty much guaranteeing Chloe's privacy *and* giving her a chance to have fun while trying on dresses."

"What?" He rested his arm between them on the back of the bench and turned partially toward her.

Zurie angled herself more toward him. "An all-girls' afternoon–slash–dress try-on party this Sunday. I sent Rina a text, and she's agreed to host it at her house. It will just be me, Rina, Philippa and Chloe, and Charlotte will stop by with dresses for us to try on."

"That definitely sounds like a better plan. It's kind of a bachelorette party."

"Maybe, or possibly closer to a bridal shower. What about Tristan? Are you planning something for him?"

"He doesn't want to do anything special. I'm sure if his two bull-riding buddies who are coming to his pseudo–birthday party were in on the wedding, things would be different. I'd like to give him some sort of send-off, though. The day of my brother's wedding, the guys gathered in his dressing room for a toast beforehand." Mace huffed a chuckle. "Efraín was so nervous, he needed that drink to settle down, but we can't do that at the pavilion. Tristan and I will just probably have drinks at the Montecito one night."

"Could you do it afterward? Maybe toward the end of the reception? Before he and Chloe leave for their honeymoon, they're changing clothes. Maybe you could quietly grab his two friends and have a toast in one of the guest rooms upstairs?"

Mace's eyes narrowed as if thinking it through. He nodded. "That could work."

"I'll arrange the room, then." Zurie grabbed her phone from her purse. "It's funny how the list of things to do keeps getting longer rather than shorter."

"I'm sorry. I didn't mean to add to it."

"No. It's not like that." She added reserving the room to her list along with checking in with Rina about how they were organizing the all-girls' afternoon party for Chloe. "What you're doing for Tristan is so important. He needs special moments just like Chloe does. I just…" The teeny voice of anxiety, the one she had to keep tamping down so it wouldn't swirl wedding details around in her mind, crept in. "I worry about dropping the ball on some small detail that will ruin their day. But I try not to think that way, because it just messes up my focus."

"Like now?"

She slipped her phone into her purse and met his gaze. Was he leaning on his general instincts about people or had she become that transparent to him? "A little."

He turned more toward her. "Do me a favor and close your eyes."

"Close my eyes? Why?"

"Just go with the flow a minute."

Was he going to try and sneak in a kiss? No. Mace understood which boundaries not to push against. He wouldn't kiss her in the middle of town square.

She obliged. "Now what?"

"Take a long meditative breath, then tell me three things you hear."

Zurie did as he asked and took a long breath in,

and as she slowly released it, she listened. "Cars, people talking…birds."

"Good. Now take another breath and tell me two things you smell." Hints of his woodsy scent wafted toward her. She'd keep that one to herself. "A bit of car exhaust…" The smell faded but was replaced with something more unpleasant. She murmured, "And someone didn't use the bags in the doggy station."

He chuckled. "You weren't the only one who noticed. It's being taken care of. Now take another breath and tell me one thing you feel."

"You mean like hungry or tired?"

"Not *how* you feel. What you sense that you're touching or is touching you."

"Oh, got it." She breathed. "The breeze on my face."

It blew strands of her hair forward on her bare shoulder. What felt like the barely there graze of Mace's fingertips gently smoothed it back. It was comforting and goose bump–raising all at the same time.

"Now open your eyes," Mace said. "Compared to a minute ago, how do you feel?"

"More relaxed." She looked to him. And even more aware of how badly she wanted to move her things out of the way, slide closer to Mace and have his arm lying on the back of the bench embrace her.

Zurie let her gaze slide away from his face to her

things on the bench. She reached for the boutique bag and her purse. "Thank you, that helped. The wine shop is open. I need to make an appointment with their sommelier to pick out wine." She rose from the bench. "What's the name of the vineyard you said I should check out? Maybe they carry their wine."

"They might. Or you could let me take you there for a long weekend." Mace rose to his feet. "It's not just a vineyard and winery. They have lodging on the property, a tasting room and a great farm-to-table menu. It's three hours away. Not too many people around here know about."

Was he suggesting what she thought he was? "You want us to spend a weekend together?"

"Yes." Mace stood in front of her. "Sitting here on the bench a minute ago, I couldn't hold your hand, and, right now, I can't kiss you goodbye because someone might see us."

Hand-holding and kisses—she wanted those things, too, but going away because of that was too risky. "I understand, but—"

"No, Zurie, I don't think you do understand. I want a chance to find out if you hog the bedsheets or if you wake up grumpy or happy in the morning. What types of songs do you sing in the shower? Do you like crispy bacon and eggs or do you prefer pancakes instead?" A man walked by them, and Mace looked down, releasing an audible breath, as he waited for them to be semialone again. When he looked back up, weariness and hints of frustration were in his eyes. "The two of us together for one long weekend, Zurie. That's all I'm asking."

Mace ran past city hall at a steady pace.

"I need time to think about it..."

That's what Zurie had told him about going away together.

Maybe he'd screwed things up between them by catching her off guard a few minutes ago and asking her that question, but he couldn't let the opportunity pass. When they'd agreed to start seeing each other, he'd tried to talk her into extending their time together until the wedding, but she'd said no. And even if he could have persuaded her to go beyond three weeks, their time would still be limited. Studying for the bar exam, giving his notice to the sheriff's department, packing up and putting his house on the market, plus finding a place in Reno, all in preparation for his big move—like Zurie, he needed to focus on the challenge ahead of him.

Efraín had called that morning to remind him of the deadline to apply to take the Nevada bar. Like he could forget. It stayed on his mind. He'd mentioned to Efraín that he was considering waiting to apply for the next exam date, a little over a year from now, and not moving to Nevada until then. That suggestion had floated as well as a rock on water. Efraín had even questioned his priorities. The bar exam,

Nevada, the family firm—they were still at the top of the list, weren't they?

Frustration fueled Mace as he veered onto the running trail just off the sidewalk shaded by trees, joining the few other joggers who were also getting a jump on the lunchtime exercise crowd.

The natural movement of his body and the breeze wicked sweat from his skin as he ran the winding path. With each stride forward, he let go of everything and cleared his mind. Three miles later the trail intersected with another one that surrounded the soccer field, basketball court and playground nestled in a grassy park. Once he completed running the oval twice, he was done. To cool off, he'd walk the short block home.

Just as he made the first curve and planned to pick up speed on the straightaway, a custom ringtone sounded in his wireless earbuds. His runner's high deflated as he slowed to a stop. It was his sister. Knowing Efraín, he'd called Andrea as soon as he'd hung up with him that morning. The tag-team effort had begun. Mace answered.

"Hey, Andrea, what's up?" Mace walked onto the grass.

"You're awake. I thought I was going to have to leave a message. You sound winded. Where are you?" The quick tapping of what sounded like high heels on tile indicated she was working. Her position as a defense attorney at a large firm in Naples, Florida, kept her busy.

"I'm out for a run. Hey, how's Justin? Did he get that promotion?"

"He's good, and yes, he got it."

"Tell him I said congrats. And Lucas. How old is he now? Seven months?"

"*¿Serio?* Are you honestly trying to distract me right now by asking me questions about your nephew? I'm calling because Efraín says you're having reservations about taking the bar exam."

"He did, huh?"

"What's the problem? Haven't you been studying?"

"No. I've been working."

"And your excuse is? You finished undergrad while you were in the marines. You went to law school part-time while working as a sheriff's deputy. You were able to study then. What's the difference now?"

Her blunt question unearthed an answer, improbable on the surface, but as he took a seat on the grass, it stood out as the truth. The drive that had gotten him through undergrad while serving in the military, and then later working as a deputy and commuting to law school in Baltimore, wasn't in him anymore when it came to becoming a lawyer.

But he couldn't admit that to Andrea. She wouldn't understand. *Driven* was her middle name.

He wiped sweat from his brow. "There isn't. I just want to make sure I'm ready."

"Don't think too long about that or you'll get stuck there. Trust me, I get it. You've had months without the weight of school on your shoulders. Getting back into studying for the bar plus working long hours can seem like climbing a mountain, but you can do it. Take some bar review courses. Get back into the habit of studying again. A couple of associates that just took it here, and passed, used a study program along with review courses to prepare for it. I'll find out which one it was and send you the information."

"Sure. I'll take a look." Whether he said yes or no, she would probably send it to him anyway.

"And remember, Efraín and I are here for whatever you need. And when it feels really difficult, just think of how proud *Mami* and especially *Papi* will be when you pass the exam and join the firm. Power through this. I know you can. I have to go. A client's waiting for me. Love you."

"Love you, too."

The call ended, but his thoughts continued. Mace closed his eyes.

"Think of how proud Mami and especially Papi will be..."

A vision of his parents, both in their early sixties, but with the energy of someone half their age, came to mind. When he'd finished law school, he'd walked across the stage for his diploma strictly for them.

The happiness reflected in their eyes and smiles had made the effort worthwhile. Afterward, he'd spent the weekend with them in DC, as well as with Andrea and her husband, Justin, and Efraín and his wife, Gia, who'd all flown in for the occasion, doing the tourist thing as a family.

He'd loved being with them those few days, but it had been a relief to return to Bolan, where no one outside of Tristan and his direct supervisor at the department knew that he'd officially completed his law school journey.

Taking time off after graduation, before studying for and then taking the bar exam, was only supposed to be a three-month pause. But three months had turned into four, then more months had suddenly slipped by him. The only thing that had kept it on his radar was his family questioning him about his plans…like now.

The reality he'd just unearthed, talking to Andrea, bore down on Mace. He hung his head. The certainty that had allowed him to know and not question if he'd take those final steps to becoming a lawyer and join his family's legacy…it wasn't there anymore. And he wasn't sure how to get it back.

Chapter Fifteen

Rina put a stack of small paper plates imprinted with blue flowers on her new white distressed coffee table in front of the cream couch.

The couch, along with matching side chairs and other furnishings, melded well in the sunlit, modern, farmhouse-themed living room decorated in hues of bright white, earthy green, beige and gray. Artfully placed nooks and corner shelves held green plants, wood-framed photos and candles. A multipatterned rug delineated the seating area on the polished floors.

The cozy space was perfect for the Sunday girls' afternoon surprise for Chloe. Everything looked great, including their coordinated outfits of dark leggings with a side pocket and blue T-shirts printed with "Bride Squad."

Zurie stood beside Rina unwrapping blue napkins. She slipped them into the caddy with the silverware. "Are you sure there's enough space for the food? Maybe we should set everything up on the dining room table."

"Having the food here will make it easier for us to enjoy. It's really not that much." Rina counted the items off on her fingers. "Mini melon and berry mozzarella skewers with yogurt dip, a veggie platter with ranch dressing, tortilla chips with guac, salsa and queso, mini chicken potpie turnovers, chocolate fondue with berries and pound cake, and if we run out of anything, I have chicken wings as a backup."

"I thought the theme was sip and dip? Drinks plus foods that you dip. What are we dipping potpie turnovers into?"

"Gravy."

"It's not gravy," Philippa called out from the adjoining kitchen, separated by a breakfast bar pass-through.

"Right, I forgot." Rina mocked a snooty voice. "It's a velvety chicken velouté, otherwise known as *fancy* gravy."

Philippa paused in stirring the contents of a pan on the stove. She looked back over her shoulder and stared at Rina. "A velouté is one of the five mother sauces in classic cuisine. It is not gravy."

Rina laughed and gave Zurie a conspiratorial wink. "Whatever you say, Chef Hoity-Toity."

Philippa pointed a spoon at Rina. "Where's the queso dip you wanted me to heat up? Did you use the fresh chiles like I told you to?"

A new debate started between the two over the right way to make queso dip.

Zurie internally shook her head as she left Rina and went into the kitchen.

Rina and Philippa had been friends for so long, they bickered like an old married couple. She tuned them out, letting the conversation slide over the surface of her thoughts as she unwrapped heavy plastic tumblers with "Drink Up" printed on the side and stacked them on the beige marble pass-through counter. She had her own pressing problem. What was her answer to Mace about going away for a long weekend?

For the past five days, she'd gone back and forth between yes and no in her mind. And Mace hadn't pressed her for an answer. Being understanding and not pressuring each other to talk about things was just one of the areas where they got along. What if going to the vineyard together actually ruined their chemistry or they just got bored being around each other for three days straight? Why risk ruining what was working for them? No. It was just working for her and not so much for Mace.

The side door of the house opened. Footsteps echoed from a back hall leading from the garage.

Scott walked into the kitchen. The blond stuntman shouldered a bag of ice and carried two small boxes of canned flavored sparkling water under his other arm. A small wet spot spread from the bag down to the front of his short-sleeved tan pullover.

Zurie hurried over to him. "I'll take those." She slipped the boxes from his hands and put them on the kitchen counter.

"Thanks." His hazel-green eyes reflected his easygoing smile. As he passed by Philippa whisking chicken stock into the pan, he peeked at what was inside. "Smells good. What are you putting gravy on?"

Rina cackled from the living room as she plumped the pillows on the couch.

Philippa gave him an indulgent smile. "It's not gravy. And I hope you're not too fond of your girlfriend, because I might have to strangle her before the day's over."

He grinned. "I do like her. So if you could refrain from doing that, I'd appreciate it."

Philippa sighed. "Well, since you asked nicely…"

As he finished tucking the ice in the bottom freezer drawer, Rina strolled in through the archway nearest to him.

He shut the door and looped an arm around Rina's waist. "The other bag of ice is in the garage freezer.

They didn't have any more lime-flavored sparkling water, so I got a grapefruit one instead."

"Perfect." Rina rose to her toes and smacked her lips to his.

They were so cute even Philippa smiled as she glanced over at them.

"Do we have an ETA on Tristan and Chloe?" Zurie asked.

It was Chloe's day off, and Rina had invited them to lunch as a way to get Chloe to the house.

"Tristan called me before they left," Scott replied. "If traffic doesn't hold them up, they should be here in about twenty minutes." He unwound his arm from Rina and dropped a kiss on her nose. "I need to change my shirt. I'm riding with Tristan back to his house." Scott left the kitchen the way Rina had come in and went upstairs.

Zurie worked with Rina and Philippa to finish setting up.

Just as Zurie and Philippa arranged the last of the food on the coffee table around the centerpiece of lavender, white and gold "Bride 2 Be" balloons, the doorbell rang.

Rina set a pitcher of spiked lemonade on the pass-through counter next to the cups and the cans of sparkling water. "Let Scott get the door." She hurried into the living room to join them by the coffee table.

Scott opened the front door that was around the corner from the living room.

Exchanged greetings echoed from the entryway along with Chloe's question. "Where's Rina?"

"She's in the living room," Scott said.

"What are we going to say when she walks in?" Rina whispered.

Philippa feigned a baffled expression. "Maybe something earth-shattering like, gee, I don't know… surprise?"

Rina bumped Philippa's arm. "Why are you my friend again?"

Happiness that their plan for Chloe had come together along with Philippa and Rina's antics pulled a laugh out of Zurie. "Philippa's actually right."

"Hey, what happened to family loyalty?" Rina interjected with a smile.

Moments later, Chloe walked around the corner. "Hey, Ri—"

The three of them shouted, throwing their hands in the air, "Surprise!"

Chapter Sixteen

Chloe's stunned expression quickly morphed into a huge smile. "Oh my gosh! What is this?"

"It's a Chloe celebration," Rina replied as she, Philippa and Zurie swarmed her with hugs.

Chloe glanced at Tristan. Lately, they seemed so much in sync, they even dressed almost alike. Her olive T-shirt and ripped jeans paired well with his khaki button-down and jeans.

"Now it makes sense." She pointed at him. "You didn't forget to bring the salad I made. You left it behind on purpose, didn't you?"

He smiled. "You can apologize for fussing at me about it later." He kissed her cheek then glanced at Scott. "We should head out. Mace is meeting us."

Hearing Mace's name snagged Zurie's attention. *He's working tonight, isn't he?* She pulled up short from calculating how many hours of sleep he may have gotten. Worrying about him. She couldn't get in the habit of doing that.

Tristan and Chloe shared a brief kiss while Scott and Rina shared a double lip smack and *I love you*s.

Scott gave a general wave as he and Tristan filed out of the living room. "Have fun, ladies."

Rina grabbed a blue gift bag with white tissue paper inside it from the couch. She held it out to Chloe. "We got you a little something to put you in the mood."

Chloe laughed. "I'm already there." She set her purse on the side chair and perched on the end of the seat. Digging through the tissue paper, she pulled out a gold "Bride 2 Be" headband and veil, a white T-shirt printed with the same wording, and dark leggings. "How cute. I'll go put them on." She hurried to the bathroom.

Philippa sat in a side chair. "So Scott and Tristan are hanging out with each other now?"

"Occasionally." Rina poured lemonade into cups. "Scott helped Tristan with a plumbing issue at his house, so they got a chance to know each other a little better, and we've had a couple of Friday date nights with them."

Zurie accepted a full cup from Rina. Date nights. If she and Mace were really a couple, they'd be part of the group. She hid disappointment behind a long sip of lemonade.

"I wonder how Tristan getting married will affect his friendship with Mace," Philippa said.

"I don't know." Rina set the pitcher back on the counter. "Maybe he'll start coming on date nights with us and bring whomever he's dating now."

"Now that's a mystery." Philippa chuckled. "Unless you believe the crazy rumor about him and Zurie."

Panic leaped in Zurie, and she coughed down the next sip of her drink. "What rumor?"

Philippa flicked her hand as if waving off an annoying bug. "Just silly gossip someone tried to float around the kitchen." She laughed. "You and Mace. Don't worry, no one believed it."

But why not her and Mace? Was it that far-fetched? The objection hovered on the tip of Zurie's tongue. Why were people so into who was dating who, anyway?

The answer was so obvious, she didn't bother saying it aloud. Bolan was growing as a town, but there were those who still had enough time and boredom on their hands to stick their nose into everyone's business and gossip about it. And that's why she shouldn't go away with Mace for the weekend. If they were both out of town at the same time, people might start putting two and two together and come up with the right answer about her and Mace.

Chloe rejoined them, and the party officially kicked off. She settled back in the middle of the couch with a plate of food and munched a mini potpie turnover drizzled with Philippa's sauce. "Wow. This is good. The chicken velouté is just right for these, not too heavy."

"Thank you for noticing." Philippa released an exaggerated breath of relief.

"I have to confess," Chloe added, dusting her fingers over her plate, "the cooking show *Dinner with Dominic* is the only reason I know what a chicken velouté is. Last time I watched his show, he was making mini chicken potpies with this sauce."

Rina leaned over from the end of the couch, grabbed a kebab and spooned yogurt dip on top of it. "Ooh, *Dinner with Dominic.* I love that show. He's delicious, and his recipes aren't bad, either."

Chloe laughed. "If you think he looks good onscreen, you should see him in person. I went to a dinner party last year where he was the chef. If I wasn't a happily engaged woman..."

"I'll have to look up his show." Zurie, sitting on the other side of Chloe, dipped a baby carrot into ranch dressing on her plate. Cooking was something Mace had mentioned might help her relax.

Philippa rose from the chair, scooped up guacamole dip with a chip and dumped it on her plate. "Dominic Crawford is an okay chef who got lucky. And I've tasted his potpie recipe. Mine is better."

Rina studied Philippa. "That's right. You've met him."

"Yes. We've met."

From the look of distaste on Philippa's face, that meeting hadn't been a good one.

Just as Rina looked ready to ask Philippa a question, the doorbell rang. "I'll get it." As she got up, she glanced at Zurie. Excitement was in Rina's eyes.

Zurie felt the same sense of anticipation.

"Is someone else coming?" Philippa asked, playing into the moment.

"Actually, it's more of a special delivery for Chloe."

Chloe paused in the midst of nibbling a kebab. "It is?"

Rina came around the corner with Charlotte.

The older woman with a silvery-blond bob, dressed in skinny jeans and a loose black long-sleeved pullover, had a timeless glow. Smiling, she walked over to Chloe. "Hello. We haven't met. I'm Charlotte Henry."

Chloe shook her hand. "Hello. We haven't met, but your name sounds familiar."

Zurie answered, "She owns Buttons & Lace, the dress shop in Bolan. She's here to help you find the right wedding dress."

Charlotte gently laid her other hand over Chloe's that was still in her hers. "Zurie showed me the dresses you were going to choose online. I found them and others that are similar, plus some other styles I think you might like. You can try them on and decide."

"Really? Like, now?" An expression of glee came over Chloe's face.

Charlotte nodded and smiled. "Right now. They're all in my van outside."

A short time later, Rina's empty downstairs guest room was transformed into a fitting room with floor-length mirrors, a rack of wedding gowns and the necessary accompaniments.

Charlotte kept things in order, using her experience and eye for detail to help quickly eliminate the styles that weren't right for Chloe.

Watching Chloe try on and model the gowns made from satin, chiffon and silk with intricate beading and lace made them all sigh and tear up a time or two.

And of course, Rina indulged her obsession with capturing memories by taking tons of pictures with her phone.

A few dresses in, Chloe tried on one of Charlotte's original creations. Zurie, along with Chloe, Rina, Philippa, was stunned into silence. This was *the* dress.

Charlotte simply nodded with a knowing smile.

Bridesmaid dresses were taken off the rack for Zurie and Rina to try on.

Chloe insisted they choose ones they would wear again.

The style they selected—a chiffon dress, with tied shoulder straps, a high-low hemline and a blue-and-peach floral pattern—was elegant enough to wear to another formal event after the wedding. Or it could be shortened so they could dress it up or dress it down for a more casual occasion in the future.

A little over two hours later, they gathered in the entryway of Rina's home to tell Charlotte goodbye.

Charlotte looked at Chloe, Rina and Zurie. "Everything worked out in our favor today. I don't have to do any major alterations on the dresses. So it's settled. We'll meet again in two weeks at Rina's old apartment for another fitting."

They all nodded. With Rina in the process of moving, it was the easiest place to meet and carry the dresses in boxes or suitcases without bringing too much attention to themselves.

Charlotte continued, "And don't forget to bring your shoes and what you plan to wear underneath the dresses and settle on how you plan to style your hair on the big day."

Zurie made a mental note. Her hair. Another important detail. Going to her usual local stylist was out of the question. The woman asked too many questions. She'd have to figure out what to do with her hair on her own.

Zurie and Rina thanked Charlotte and hugged her goodbye.

Chloe walked out with Charlotte, carting a rolling bag of supplies out to the van. Once the bag was loaded inside, the two women hugged each other like newfound friends and continued talking.

As Rina and Zurie looked on from the doorway, Rina slipped her arm through Zurie's and gave her a nudge. "You've given Chloe some great memories today."

Zurie nudged Rina back. "We've given her some great memories."

"I was just following your lead on a great plan." Rina slipped her hand away, partially closed the front door and headed for the kitchen to help Philippa clean up. "Take the credit. You done good."

Taking credit wasn't important. Chloe having happy, memorable moments leading up to the wedding was. And, honestly, that afternoon, trying on dresses, might not have happened without Mace's input.

Giving in to the sudden urge, Zurie slipped down the hallway to the unfurnished, beige-carpeted guest room. Through the window facing the front yard, she could see Charlotte and Chloe still talking in the driveway.

She slipped her phone from the side pocket of her leggings and called Mace's number.

He picked up on the fourth ring. "Hello. Hold on a minute."

Tristan's voice filtered in from the background.

Shoot. That's right. Mace couldn't just take her call. He had to go someplace private.

Moments later, he came back on the line. "Okay. I can talk now."

What she'd planned to tell him suddenly seemed small compared to the effort he'd just made to take her call. "I just wanted to tell you everything went well here."

"I'm glad to hear it."

"What you said about your sister having a bonding moment trying on dresses, that helped. A lot. Thank you."

"You're welcome. I'm here to help."

He really had helped her a lot with the wedding planning, and, so far, he'd only asked her for one thing.

Zurie tamped down the part of her that caused her to overanalyze things. "I don't sing in the shower. I like my bacon crispy but not burned. I'm not crazy about eggs, but I'll eat them. And I like waffles topped with warm syrup and butter. And as far as the rest of what you wanted to know, you'll have to find out yourself...when we're at the vineyard."

Chapter Seventeen

Zurie slipped a neatly folded pink T-shirt into the blue paisley travel bag sitting on her bed. Now she was ready. Hopefully her long weekend with Mace would pass as slowly as the time had since she'd agreed to go with him. Four days of continued anticipation had almost driven her nuts. But thankfully, her caffeine withdrawal headaches had subsided and she could fully enjoy the wine-tasting experience that weekend.

Her phone rang on the nightstand, and she glanced at the screen. *Mace.* He'd texted her that morning, confirming they were leaving at 10:00 a.m. for the Sommersby Farm Vineyard and Winery. That was in a couple of hours. Why was he calling her now?

She answered, “Hi.”

“I’m at the store buying snacks for the road. Do you want anything in particular?”

“It’s only a three-hour car ride. I’ll be fine.”

“Okay. Just don’t be offended if I won’t share my gummi bears with you.”

“Gummi bears, huh?” The thought of him hoarding the bag of candy made her smile. She could probably convince him to give her a few. “Regular or the sour ones?”

“I was thinking of getting one each.”

“Get two of the sour ones.”

He chuckled. “I knew you’d see things my way about snacks. I think I saw some on the other aisle. There’s a place on the way that makes wood-fired pizza. I thought we could stop there for lunch or would you rather bring something?”

“The pizza place sounds good. Can you grab drinks?” She named the brand she wanted.

“On it. And I’ve got water for us, too. So I think that’s it. We’re ready.”

“Yep.” Flutters of excitement loosed inside her.

“See you at the house.”

Just as she went to slip the phone into the side pocket of her bag, a call rang in. It was probably Mace again.

She answered without checking the screen. “If you’re calling to ask if I’ll share my sour gummis, I will if it’s an even trade.”

"Uh, no, that wasn't why I was calling."

Crap. Not Mace. It was Tristan. A small laugh escaped Zurie. "I thought you were someone else."

"So I guess you're busy?"

The dejected tone in his voice snared her attention. "No. I'm free. What's going on."

"I have a problem." His long exhale filled the silence. "I lost Chloe's engagement ring."

Zurie's heart dropped. "What? When?"

"Sometime yesterday afternoon. Chloe accidentally brought the ring with her to the set, and I picked it up from her. I stuck it in my pocket, went to the office and got busy. I forgot I had it. Chloe got home late last night and didn't ask me about it until this morning on her way out the door. I couldn't tell her I didn't know where her ring was. I'm retracing my steps starting with here at the house."

"Do you want me to come help you look for it?"

"Actually, I was hoping you could take care of something else for me. Anna Ashford is supposed to interview me this morning. She'll be at the office in about twenty minutes, and Gloria's off today."

"Don't worry. I'll handle the interview. Is there anything else I can do? Do I need to check on the staff?"

"The stable is fine. Blake is in charge. Could you look around my desk for the ring? Damn. I can't believe I messed up this bad. If I can't find it, I'll give Chloe two engagement rings if she'll forgive me."

He sounded miserable, and Zurie's heart went out to him. "Don't give up. I'll take care of Anna and look around the office."

"Thanks."

After she hung up, Zurie's gaze landed on her travel bag. If Tristan didn't find the ring, she couldn't just leave town and abandon him. The reason he was so busy was because he was doing her job as well as his own. She had to pitch in and help find the ring.

Zurie grabbed her ID case and keys from her purse, which was inside the travel bag, slipped her feet into the wedge-heeled sandals by the bed and rushed out of the suite. Her jeans and black T-shirt would just have to be good enough for the interview. Hopefully Anna wouldn't take pictures of her.

A short time later, at the entrance to the paved parking lot behind the large horse stable, the guard recognized Zurie and waved her inside.

Having increased security on the property because of the film was still a bit strange.

After parking in a vacant space in the half-empty parking lot, she stuck the ID case in the middle console, grabbed her phone and got out.

A dappled gray horse and two bays were on the closest end of the adjoining paddock on the right of the stable. On the far end, a groom raked and cleaned the area. The pungent smells of horses, hay and grass were in the air.

Anna's blue four-door wasn't in the parking lot yet.

Good. Zurie used the key fob to lock her car and hurried from the parking lot to the paved narrow path leading to the back side door of the stable. She had at least a good five to ten minutes to look around for the ring in the office before the interview.

She unlocked the door and walked into the light-tiled hallway. To the right, up ahead, black- and silver-framed photos hung on the walls. Voices and the brays and whinnies of horses echoed from the interior of the modern stable farther down.

A few of the horses were looking out the top part of the horizontally split navy Dutch-style doors, watching the comings and goings of people and other horses being led up and down the wide rubber-floored aisle.

Trainers were headed for the outdoor exercise ring while locals who boarded their horses at the stable were saddling up for rides.

At this time of the day, Blake would double-check that the stalls were in order along with the tack room. He'd also make sure they were ready to conduct afternoon horse-riding lessons, tours and trail rides for guests staying at the guesthouse.

Zurie unlocked the door in front of her and walked into the beige-tiled white-walled space Tristan shared with Gloria, the stable's office administrator.

Smart windows along the wall on the left had darkened to a smoky blue gray, keeping the office cool and letting in light. Zurie flipped the switch on the wall, fully illuminating the office.

She walked past Gloria's wood-topped metal desk on the right. All of Gloria's papers and files had been stored, and only her wide-screen desktop computer and a caddy with pens and desk supplies sat on top of it.

Tristan's wood desk was the opposite, with several stacks of files, papers, a tube of horse liniment and sample packages of horse treats that a company rep had probably dropped off.

Zurie looked around and underneath the desk first. Nothing but a couple of stray paper clips.

She set her phone near the desktop computer and searched the desk. As she shifted things around, a stack of papers and packages of treats slid to the floor. What looked like a mess to her was Tristan's organized chaos. She didn't want to disturb things too much, or maybe he wouldn't care if she did since finding the ring was a priority. Either way, she was going to have to wait until after the interview to really move things around and look.

Her phone buzzed, and she checked the screen before picking it up. It was Mace.

"Hi." She picked up the fallen papers and bags of treats.

"Hey. I was wondering. I got all my errands done. How do you feel about leaving a little earlier?"

A knock sounded on the open door.

Anna stood in the hallway.

"Hold on," Zurie said to Mace. Smiling politely, she waved the late-thirties blonde inside the office. "Hi, Anna. Come in and have a seat." Zurie gestured to the chairs in front of Tristan's desk.

"Hello." Anna walked in. Her navy blazer with pushed-up sleeves over a T-shirt and cream beige chinos looked casual but screamed expensive. And so were her artfully worn brown ankle boots.

A tinge of admiration for Anna's outfit intertwined with Zurie feeling underdressed in comparison. "We may have to alter our plans. Something has come up."

"Alter as in we can't go?"

Anna took her time, setting her large tan bag in the chair. She tucked a strand of her long hair behind her ear and cocked her head as if listening to the phone conversation.

"Hold on." Zurie held the phone to her chest, muffling her conversation with Anna. She pointed to the beverage station in the corner. "There should be water and juices in the fridge. Feel free to grab something. I'll be done in minute."

"Is Tristan joining us?"

"No, I'm afraid not. Something unexpected that he really had to attend to came up. I'm taking his place for the interview."

"But I was expecting to talk to him. Why didn't

Gloria call me about the change before I drove all the way out here?"

"It's been a little hectic today, and we didn't want to hold you up from publishing your article by rescheduling. Your questions are about the new indoor arena, right? Or did the mayor misunderstand you?"

Anna didn't even try to disguise her annoyance. "Well, yes."

"Then we're good." Zurie pasted on a slight smile. "Just let me finish up this call, and I can answer all your questions."

She went out of the office, shut the door behind her and went out the side door. "Sorry about that. I'm back."

"I couldn't hear everything, but your tone during that conversation didn't sound vacation friendly. Are you at work? What happened?"

"That was just Anna Ashford." Zurie let go of irritation. "I'm at the stable in Tristan's office, but I'm not working. Just subbing in on an interview she was supposed to do with Tristan. He couldn't do it because he lost Chloe's engagement ring."

She filled him on the details.

"Damn, that's rough," Mace said. "He spent a lot of time searching for the right ring. I know he's probably beating himself up about. Yeah, we can't leave him like this. I'll head out there now and give him a hand."

Gratefulness went through her. Of course Mace

would understand. "Once Anna leaves. I'll take the office apart. If I don't find it, I'll meet you there."

"Hopefully you won't have to. Aside from the office, you may want to retrace his steps from the stable to the parking lot. It's a long shot, but sometimes things turn up in the places you don't expect to find them."

"I will.

"And good luck with Anna. I heard she's persistent. My bosses at the department avoid talking to her."

"I can handle her. And thank you."

"For what, wishing you luck or buying you gummi bears?"

"For being you." She didn't have to see him to imagine his smile.

"You can thank me later. After we find Chloe's ring. 'Bye."

She ended the call. Just as Zurie reached to open the door, she paused, taking Mace's advice to glance around the small concrete landing and the grass immediately surrounding it. Nothing shiny stood out. If only she had time to check the path. And she needed to find out where Tristan had parked his SUV yesterday. But she needed to deal with Anna first.

Zurie walked inside the office and sat behind Tristan's desk.

"Do you mind if I record?" Anna held up her phone. "That way I don't have to write so much."

"Sure. So, let's talk about the new indoor arena."

Anna gave a relaxed smile, crossed her legs and sat back in the chair with a pen and notepad. "Yes, let's talk about that."

Over the next forty minutes, Anna surprisingly asked questions strictly about the stable and the plans for new arena.

Maybe it was better that Tristan hadn't done the interview. Anna was staying on task.

Anna flipped through her notes. "I think that's it except for one more question. The love triangle that Tristan is in the midst of with Chloe Daniels and Nash Moreland—any updates about that?"

So now the fishing expedition. Too bad Anna was about to come up short. "It's a silly rumor that we're not going comment on. If you have more questions about the arena or Tillbridge Horse Stable and Guesthouse, I'm happy to answer them."

The side door opened.

As Tristan and Mace peeked into the office, Tristan's grim expression and Mace's empathetic one told her all she needed to know.

Anna glanced over her shoulder. "Tristan, I'm glad you could make it."

He pointed down the hall. "Actually, something urgent has come up that I need to look into. I'm sure Zurie's filled you in on everything you need to know."

"Oh, not everything." Anna put her pen and notepad into her tote sitting on the chair beside her. She pulled out Chloe's engagement ring and held it up. "I found this under your desk." With a self-satisfied smile, she glanced at Zurie, then Tristan. "Care to comment?"

Chapter Eighteen

Anna had had the ring the entire time of the interview? Zurie sprang from her seat at the same time Tristan and Mace walked into the office.

As she rounded the desk, she caught a glimpse of Tristan's face and his forthcoming confession. It wasn't fair for him and Chloe to have their happiness ruined. She couldn't let him do it.

He went to speak, but Zurie interrupted him. "It's mine."

Anna blinked back at her. "Yours?" She laughed. "We all know that's not true."

The slight slipped through, hitting a place inside Zurie that made her pause in reaching for the ring.

"It is true." Mace came forward, emanating confidence. Anna's laughing smile disappeared as he slipped the ring from her grasp and went to Zurie. "It just happened a few days ago. We're planning to make the announcement after the filming of the movie is over and the stable is back to normal."

As he slid the diamond on Zurie's ring finger, the weight of the ring and a weird excitement hit her at the same time.

Once the diamond was in place, he held Zurie's hand and her gaze. "We need to get this resized, *mi amor.* It keeps slipping off your finger. We're really lucky Anna found it."

Her heart sped up as he kissed the back of her hand. "Yes, we're very lucky. But that's why I brought it with me. I thought we could take it to the jeweler's today."

"Oh, no." Anna shook her head and pointed at Mace. "You were dating two other women up until at least a month ago."

"Circumstances change," Mace said. "If you don't believe me, I'll show you my credit card receipt for the ring—if it'll stop you from selling whatever false story you planned on cooking up about Tristan and Chloe."

Anna's eyes widened slightly before her expression turned smug. "If I were selling a story somewhere, that's not a crime."

The crime was Anna believing it was her job to

turn Tristan and Chloe's personal life into entertainment when that's not what they wanted. Zurie tamped down anger. "No, it's not, but I'm not sure the mayor would be on board with his sister-in-law spreading false stories about a member of his community."

"Yeah, that probably wouldn't go down well," Tristan added, taking a seat behind his desk. "Especially if he's looking to get reelected."

Anna looked from Tristan to Zurie to Mace as if calculating the value of the information she had. And what she didn't.

She rose from the chair. "It's a busy day. I have to get to my next appointment." Her smile didn't veil the condescension in her eyes. "I'll be in touch to see when it's a good time for the photographer to stop by and take pictures of the new arena. I can't wait to share about it." Her gaze landed on Zurie and Mace. "Or your impending nuptials once you decide to make the announcement." She walked toward the door.

"Anna," Tristan called out, and she turned around. "Your phone." He pointed to where it lay on his desk.

"Oh. I completely forgot." Her cheeks grew pink as she went back and snatched it from the desk. Turning up her nose, she stomped out.

The outer door shut, and as Zurie thought about the bullet they'd just dodged, she leaned on Mace.

"Good thing you caught that. Her phone was on record. She probably left it behind on purpose."

"I can't believe her." Tristan lifted his hand and dropped it on his desk. "If I didn't know any better, I'd swear Anna was related to my dad's ex-wife. Do you think she bought it?"

"Doesn't matter if she did or not," Mace replied. "The key is she knows we're on to her."

"Thanks for jumping in like that—both of you." Tristan gave a nod their directions.

"That's what we're here for. Nothing's going to stop your wedding." Zurie released Mace's hand. She went around the desk to Tristan, slipped off the platinum band with the sparkling diamond and handed it to him.

He stared down at the ring. "Maybe we should call the ceremony and reception off. Planning a secret wedding is one thing, but forcing you to keep pretending you're engaged like you did in front of Anna, that's too much to ask."

The sadness on Tristan's face contrasted sharply with her memory of his happiness at the pavilion as he'd envisioned getting married there. And of Chloe's glee at the party, trying on dresses.

Zurie looked to Mace. Staying together longer and pretending to be engaged until the wedding wasn't that much of a hardship…was it?

As if he'd read her mind, Mace nodded.

Zurie walked over to him, and as he held out his

hand, she took it. The firmness of his grasp conveyed what she felt. They were in this together—saving the wedding, making sure Chloe and Tristan had their day…and revealing their own secret.

She faced Tristan. "No, it's not too much to ask."

Tristan opened his mouth as if to object, but he remained speechless as she and Mace intertwined their fingers. His brow raised. "You two are together? Since when?"

Mace answered, "Since we started planning your wedding."

She jumped in, answering the questions reflected in Tristan's face. "No one knows. I've always kept my personal life private, and Mace agreed to honor that. It also didn't make sense to tell anyone because we're only together for a few weeks."

"Okay. I wasn't expecting this." Tristan sat back in the chair. "I guess what matters is that you're both good with what's happening. You know what you're doing." He looked at both of them, but his gaze stayed on Mace a beat longer.

Mace looked back at him. "Everything's under control."

Zurie picked up the subtle undercurrent in the room. This wasn't about her. The two needed to talk as friends.

She spoke to Tristan. "Yes, everything *is* under control. We all just have to maintain what we're doing until the wedding, and that's only three weeks away. Don't worry about us. Just put that ring in a safe place." Zurie looked to Mace. "I'll meet you at the guesthouse?"

"Yes, I'll see you there."

Mace kissed Zurie on the cheek. Before he let go of her, he gave her hand a squeeze to let her know that things were still good.

Zurie gave him a soft smile.

Her moving out of her comfort zone to help Tristan and Chloe wasn't surprising, but after Zurie acted on impulse, she tended to let things get into her head. Luckily, they had whole long weekend to sort through her worries together.

The door clicked shut behind her.

Mace sat in the chair in front of Tristan's desk. "I know you're not worried about how I'll treat Zurie. So what else is on your mind?"

"You're right, I'm not worried, because you know if you did hurt her, I would find you and feed you to the wolves. What I am concerned about is what you and Zurie are doing. It's really easy for feelings to get involved."

Tristan didn't have to finish saying what he was thinking. Mace understood. When feelings got too involved, people got hurt. "If it starts to look like it's becoming a problem for Zurie, I'll make sure we work it out."

"Zurie?" Tristan huffed a chuckle. "I'm not worried about her. I'm worried about you."

"Me? Why?"

"A couple of months ago, when I was twisted up over my relationship with Chloe, you were sitting in that very chair when you told me that if you could be with the woman you wanted to be with, you would."

"And you think I meant Zurie?"

Tristan gave up a shrug. "You tell me."

"I think you're reading way more into what I said. Back then, it was obvious you wanted to be with Chloe, but you were too afraid to admit it at first. I was just trying to wake you up to the fact you didn't want to lose her over some boneheaded decision you made."

"You're right. And I'm glad you were there to help me see it. I'm trying to do the same for you." Tristan leaned forward on the desk. "A short-term thing plus pretending to be engaged—things could get complicated…for all of us." He looked Mace in the eye. "Don't make my wedding present having to choose between family or my best friend."

Mace parked just past the front of the guesthouse.

Zurie walked out the front door and down the porch steps, sunglasses on the top of her head, wheeling a paisley-blue travel duffel behind her.

He'd sent her a text before he'd left the stable a few minutes ago, after assuring Tristan his points were noted but not a concern. He wasn't going to put Tristan in the position of having to choose between keeping his friendship with him or loyalty to family.

He got out, and by the time he'd walked to the front passenger side, she'd reached him.

"Everything okay?" she asked. The smile she gave him rated less than passable on the happiness scale.

"Tristan and I are good." Mace slipped the handle of the bag from her hand, collapsed it and put her bag on the back seat with his duffel and the cooler he'd packed with their drinks. "But you're not." He shut the door.

"No, I'm fine."

Mace took her by the waist and gently pulled her into a loose embrace. "You don't have to pretend with me. What's going on in your head right now?"

Bracing for her to pull away because they were in public, she surprised him by laying her hands near his shoulders. The sadness in her eyes caused a strange tug in his chest. "I almost ruined Tristan and Chloe's wedding day. I never should have left Anna alone in Tristan's office."

"No. You don't get to do that. You don't get to take responsibility or assign blame for someone else's screwed-up actions. What Anna did was wrong. What you *do* get to do is remember how you, Tristan and I solved the problem."

"Did we? Or did we just add on another one? We're fake engaged. You know Anna isn't going to keep it a secret. She'll tell everyone out of spite because we embarrassed her. By the time we get back, it will be all over town."

"And I like it, because now we don't have to pretend in public that we don't like each other."

"But—"

Mace captured her mouth, and her lips curved into a smile under his. She leaned away slightly. "You're just going to keep doing that if I keep talking about this, aren't you?"

"Yep. If we have to talk about it, I'd rather do it at the vineyard, drinking wine, eating great food and having a good time watching a movie under the stars."

"They have an outdoor theater?" Her eyes lit up.

"Sort of." He released her and opened the front passenger side door. "But you won't get to find out about that, along with all other great things they have, if we don't leave."

Before she stepped up into the truck, she kissed his cheek.

"What was that for?"

"Just trying out the whole PDA thing."

Glad to see humor in her eyes, he was anxious to get underway. "You'll get lots of practice this weekend."

Chapter Nineteen

A little over three hours after the start of their road trip, Zurie opened the front passenger side window, eager to get a closer look at the view.

Mace looked over at her and smiled. “What do you think?”

“It’s beautiful.”

Sommersby’s simple website hadn’t quite captured what unfolded in front of her. Rows of grapevines nestled in a valley of lush green trees under a blue sky with dashes and puffs of soft white clouds.

The breeze drifting over her skin held hints of coolness and warmth. Instead of the earthy smell of horses, it was filled with the scents of rich soil, lush plants, green grass and hints of a sweetness from flowering bushes lining the road.

From what she'd briefly read about the place online, it was a family-owned operation, like Tillbridge, and had been around for generations. It had started out as a farm with livestock, and over the past ten years had transitioned into a vineyard and winery. They also maintained a small orchard and grew a few seasonal vegetables.

They entertained only a few overnight guests at a time in their four-room lodging house, which was open just Friday through Sunday to the general public.

It was the perfect place to unwind and unplug. She and Mace had agreed to go all in on the unplug part of things. Neither one of them had packed a computer tablet or a laptop, and they were taking a break from their phones. They would check for voice mails and texts in the morning. Outside of that, no calls. No social media checks. If there was an emergency back at Tillbridge or something that concerned Mace, Tristan knew where to reach them and so did Kayla.

Mace slowed down as the road curved. Back on the straightaway, they drove past a large red building with white trim designed like a barn with a double-pitched metal roof complete with a weather vane at its peak. A wraparound porch decorated with floral arrangements in metal pitchers on top of wine barrels awaited occupants to sit and take in the view of an open lawn from Adirondack and wood rocking chairs.

"What building is that?" she asked.

"The winery and tasting room."

At the end of the road, a sign pointed right to Summer House Lodge.

He turned left.

She pointed back at the sign. "Lodging is that way."

"I know."

A short distance later, he turned off the road. Farther back in the trees sat a small, modest white house with a red door and trim.

Mace parked in front of it. "This is where we're staying. Come on. Let's check it out. Leave the bags. I'll come back for them."

"Don't we need a key?"

"They use remote check-in." At the door, Mace keyed the code into the pad above the lock.

As soon as the door opened, she was drawn into the white-walled space with dark wood ceiling beams and trim. A king-size bed with built-in wood headboard sat to the right. On the left, a high black marble counter sectioned off the corner kitchen. Next to it was small wood kitchen table with four chairs. On the other end, a brick fireplace with an ottoman and russet side chairs formed a cozy seating area.

He shut the door behind them. "What do you think?"

Pleasant surprise and excitement made her smile. "It's wonderful. I didn't see anything about this on Sommersby's website."

"They don't really advertise it, but they actually have two cottages on the property."

Mace opened the back door, and they walked out onto a wood deck surrounded by a low railing.

Zurie couldn't stop smiling as she took in the vineyard and the green hills beyond.

He pointed. "In front of us is one of the sections where the grapes are grown. To the left, where the rows look similar, that's actually part of the apple orchard. The trees are grown in the espalier method."

"What's that?"

"The trees are trained to grow on a frame instead of freestanding. They also grow olives and make their own olive oil. I don't think we can see that from here. You have to get their *insalata caprese*. The tomatoes, basil and olive oil come from here, and the mozzarella is from a local dairy."

"You really know a lot about this place."

"But not everything. They have all kinds of hidden surprises." Mace embraced her from behind, and she leaned back against him. "I learned about the cottages the last time I stayed here."

The last time... He'd probably been there with someone else. Happiness deflated a little inside her.

Mace kissed her temple. "Instead of guessing, you could just ask me what you want to know."

Wow. She really was that transparent to him. "There's no point in asking. You weren't a monk before we started seeing each other. I know that."

"I've been here three times—on my own. I discovered this place the first time by accident when I had to take a detour on the way back from driving to New York. The second time, I came out here for the day after a rough week at work. The third time was about a month ago. You're tensing up. You don't believe me?"

Note to self: she needed to never play poker with Mace or get much better at hiding her thoughts. "I do believe you. You coming out here by yourself instead of with someone or a group of people is just a little…surprising."

He held her tighter. "Is that a bad thing?"

Like the vineyard revealed surprises to Mace, he revealed them to her about himself. The more she discovered, the more she wanted to be with him.

"No, it isn't." She snuggled back in his arms. "How in the world did you get this cottage on such short notice? Isn't it booked out way in advance?"

"Yes. Usually it is. But they had a last-minute cancellation. When I called this morning to let them know we might arrive later than expected, they offered it to me at a discount." He chuckled. "It wasn't intentional, but it kind of fits in with our fake engagement."

She glanced back at him over her shoulder. "Back

in Tristan's office, when we were getting fake engaged. You said *mi amor.* That means my love, doesn't it?"

"Yes, literally, that's what it means. But it can also mean honey or sweetheart."

"And if I'm remembering my high school Spanish correctly, fiancée is *novia*?"

"No. *Novia* means girlfriend." He pointed to her. "*Tu eres mi prometida.*" He pointed to himself. "*Yo soy tu prometido.*"

She chuckled ruefully. "If we're going to pull off this fake engagement, I guess I better brush up on my Spanish. So, have you ever had a real *prometida*?"

"First, great pronunciation. And no. I've never been engaged. You're my first. What about you?" He gave her a squeeze. "Have you ever been engaged?"

"Let's see…" She silently counted numbers on her fingers.

When she got past three, he spun her around by the waist to face him. "You've been engaged four times?"

"Um." The stunned expression on his face made it impossible to keep in a laugh. "No, I'm kidding, just once."

"So you really were engaged?" He studied her face. "Tristan had never mentioned it. When was this?"

As it did a minute ago, Zurie's silence spoke as loud as words to him. The way she fiddled with the small gold loop in her earlobe and released a heavy exhale now in his arms, those were her major tells.

As he debated between waiting for an answer or suggesting they check out what tours were available that afternoon, she looked up at him. "About seven years ago. His name was Theo. We met when he and his colleagues visited the stable. We connected. Managed to work out the long-distance part of things with him in New York… In time, things got serious." She dropped her gaze.

"He proposed, and I said yes. But a month later, he was offered a better job in Dallas. It was an opportunity he'd really wanted. And to get where he wanted to go in his career, he needed all his attention there. Not on building a relationship. By then, we had started drifting apart. And I had Tillbridge to worry about. No one really knew about him and we hadn't announced our engagement, so were able to end things quietly."

The job opportunity was what Theo had really wanted? Why had the guy bothered to propose to her in the first place if she wasn't a priority to him? Irritation on her behalf wove through Mace. Had her family known about Theo, maybe they would have bounced the guy out before he hurt her. But seven years ago, Tristan had still been in the military. Her father and uncle had been alive, but wasn't that around the time Rina had eloped to Nevada? Knowing Zurie, she'd not only quietly ended her engagement but also quietly endured the pain, prioritizing being there for her family first.

Mace slid his hands from the sides of Zurie's waist to her back, bringing her closer. "I'm sorry that happened to you. From where I stand, if his job was more important than you, it was probably better that he moved on and out of your life."

She laid her left hand on his chest as she looked up at him. "It was. I know that now."

As he looked down at her, the recollection of slipping the ring on Zurie's finger in Tristan's office that morning came into his mind. When Anna had laughed as if were impossible for Zurie to have anyone, it had ticked him off. And from Zurie's expression in that moment, she'd seen Anna's take on her as the truth. Claiming the ring and slipping it on Zurie's finger, he'd done it for Tristan and Chloe, but he'd also wanted to erase the smug look on Anna's face and the stunned hurt on Zurie's. And he'd succeeded at both.

Zurie stared at her hand on his chest. "I really hope Tristan takes a minute to drive home and put Chloe's ring away."

Funny. She'd been thinking of the ring, too. "That's definitely on his agenda. Along with straightening the house. He'd torn through most of the rooms before I got there to help him look. It's messed up that Anna was the one to find the ring, but I'm glad she did. At the house, when Tristan had finally decided to give up and retrace his steps back to Tillbridge to keep looking, he was pretty devastated. I've seen him at low points before in his life, but this was different."

"I know what you mean. He was really disappointed in himself and worried about letting Chloe down. I recently complained about him smiling all the time lately, but I'll gladly take that over seeing him like he was this morning."

"You complained about him smiling?"

"Kind of, but not really." Chuckling, she nudged his arm. "Stop looking at me like that. I know it sounds terrible. It's just weird and wonderful at the same time, seeing him with a goofy I'm-in-love grin on his face. For some reason it reminds of when he was five years old. He used to run around in Superman pj's with a red towel for a cape, excited about the dollar the Tooth Fairy had left him under his pillow."

A laugh escaped Mace.

Zurie playfully wacked him. "Don't you dare tell him I told you about that."

"Why would I?" Mace laughed. Yeah, Tristan wearing Superman pj's was definitely something he'd bring up when Tristan least expected it. But now was the time for them to enjoy themselves.

He glided his hands up and down her back, enjoying the freedom to just hold her without restrictions. “We can still make the afternoon tour of the vineyard and winery if you’re interested.”

A pleased smile lit up Zurie’s face. “Let’s do it.”

Chapter Twenty

The tour of the vineyard, learning about the careful process of nurturing the grapes currently ripening on the vine. The visit to the winery to learn about the process of producing and aging wine. Time with the vintner experiencing the first pour from a barrel, comparing it to the current vintage and tasting how the wine would evolve. Mace was there for every moment that had happened yesterday, but he barely remembered them.

He'd been captivated by the relaxed softness in Zurie's face, the slight furrow in her brow as she contemplated the differences in the wine they'd sampled and the subtle widening of her eyes when she'd tasted something she really liked. The smile on her face as they'd walked the paths to the vineyards had warmed him more than the sun.

That Saturday morning she'd bitten into a fresh peach in the orchard. A rich, bubbling laugh had erupted from her, and he'd been undone by the beauty of the sound. And the look in her eyes when she'd offered him a bite had caused him to bypass the fruit and go straight to her mouth for a taste of sweetness.

Time was going by too fast. They were headed home tomorrow.

Mace absorbed the reality of that, sitting on a blanket with Zurie on the lawn just past the restaurant in the Summer House Lodge.

Almost every table on the wood patio attached to the simply built, two-story white clapboard structure was full with patrons enjoying food, wine and conversation. The lawn was dotted with couples sitting on blankets enjoying an intimate picnic under the stars.

In less than a half hour, the mystery-comedy movie *Knives Out* would play on the screen yards away from them.

Mace added more *insalata caprese* to his smaller plate from the one sitting in front of them, along with a slice of herbed chickpea bruschetta.

Instead of eating the food on her plate, Zurie glanced around them, absently swirling her glass of rosé. In a simple beige tee and pink shorts, with her hair in a single braid, she looked comfortable and at ease with herself.

Mace took a bite of the *insalata*. The blend of fresh tomatoes, mozzarella and basil with olive oil and a light sprinkling of oregano was as delicious as when they'd had it on Friday.

A server dropping off a basket of warm crostini and crackers for the fig and olive tapenade shifted Zurie's attention back to the food. She slipped her wineglass into the wood holder that also had a carved-out section to hold the bottle of wine. "I could just eat this alone and be satisfied. It's so good."

Mace took a bite of crostini with the tapenade.

"I was starting to wonder if you liked it. You're not really eating, just staring out there. Do you see something or are you looking for something?"

"Maybe a bit of both." Smiling, she brushed crumbs from the bottom of his black T-shirt and then his bare thigh just below the leg of his beige cargo shorts. "With your brother and sister being married, do you ever feel like you're behind in the relationship department?"

It didn't sound like she was questioning him but trying to work out something in her own mind. Was that how she felt with Tristan getting married and Rina being in a serious relationship?

Instead of indulging his curiosity over the source of the question, Mace summed up his dating relationships over the past few years in his mind. "No, I don't feel behind. My circumstances have just been different from theirs. When I was in the military, the first four years, I wasn't interested in getting into anything serious. The last four years, multiple deployments made it hard to maintain a relationship. Afterward, finishing law school took up most of time."

She whipped her head around and looked at him. "Wait. You finished law school? When?"

"Last year. Didn't I mention it?" They'd talked about so many things that weekend, he honestly thought he had.

"No. I would have remembered. How am I just hearing about this now instead of when it happened?"

"We weren't exactly communicating back then."

Something bordering on regret passed over her face.

He hadn't said that to make her feel bad. Mace placed his hand over hers, resting on her thigh. "Outside of my family, Tristan and few people at work, no one else really knew."

"But becoming a lawyer, that's a big deal. Your dad's a lawyer. Your brother's a lawyer."

"My sister is, too."

"See? It's the family business. Are you planning to leave the sheriff's department and work at a law firm?"

"I haven't even applied to take the bar exam yet."

"When are you planning to do it?"

The familiar question pinged around his mind as he scooped up more tapenade with a cracker.

After he'd spoken to Andrea that day in the park, he'd printed out the instructions document for the bar exam in Nevada. The list of things he'd needed to pull together was long—his college transcripts, DMV report, letters of reference and his military discharge papers. And Andrea hadn't just found out the info on the study system, she'd sent it to him. Admittedly, it would be a complement to the review course he'd signed up for online. Everything was in motion. He just needed to get his head back into it.

But he'd figure out how to do that once he got home.

Zurie waited for an answer.

He handed her the cracker. "I'm taking it when the time is right. And right now, we're not supposed to talk about anything work related, remember?"

"Yes, I remember." Her mouth flattened as if she was stopping herself from blurting something out. She nibbled on the cracker with tapenade. When she finished, she looked out at the vineyard and released a barely audible sigh.

Where was on her mind now? They had less than twenty-fours left together. The two of them together, right then, that's where her attention should have been.

Mace leaned over, pressed a kiss near her ear and

whispered, "If you're thinking about Tillbridge, stop. If you're trying to compute the distance to Mars or the formula for gravity boots in your head, double stop. If you're thinking about me becoming a lawyer, stop. Whatever you're thinking about, it can wait until you get back."

"Okay. Fine. I'll stop." She gave him a playful eye roll. "The formula for gravity boots? Please, that's too easy. I could do that one in my sleep."

"Yeah, I bet you could, Miss Smarty-Pants." He poked a sensitive spot on her side.

Laughing, she batted his hand away. "Now you stop. Remember how the last tickle war you started with me ended?"

Yesterday morning, he'd started it as they'd made the bed. Zurie had ended it later during breakfast. She'd caught him off guard while he was drinking orange juice, and he'd snorted some up his nose.

Mace wrapped an arm around her from behind. "For the record, that was an unfair sneak attack."

Smiling, she shrugged. "Oh, well." Her smile faded slightly as she leaned into him. "I wasn't thinking of Tillbridge, not in the way you're thinking. It's just interesting to me—at Tillbridge, the priorities are filling the cottages and rooms at the guesthouse, booking every table at Pasture Lane and every slot possible at the stable. Here, it's different. Their focus is that." She pointed out at the vineyards surrounding them.

"You think it should be different?"

"No. It's just so...fragile. If Mother Nature is in a bad mood and there's too much rain, wind or frost, the vineyard is in danger. In my opinion, that's a frightening position to be in." A slightly puzzled, faraway look came over her face. "The day after Uncle Jacob died, I walked through every pasture. All that was out there was just me and the horses. As I looked around and thought about not losing what he and my parents had built, I realized that the horses and I weren't enough. That's when I decided to build the guesthouse and Pasture Lane Restaurant." She gave a quick smile that fell short of true happiness. "And that's why I'm not in charge of an agricultural enterprise. I'm obviously not cut out for it."

For a brief moment, Mace glimpsed the vulnerability in her that she'd experienced back then. Something she'd probably started masking from the world, the moment she'd lost her mother almost ten years ago and then her father a few years after, and through Rina and Tristan both not being at Tillbridge or able to help her.

Empathy unexpectedly welled inside him. Mace pulled her close, and as he pressed a lingering kiss to her temple, he breathed in her lavender and vanilla scent. She'd carried all that on her young shoulders and succeeded. But what had it cost her?

After the movie, as they walked into the cottage,

Mace couldn't shake what Zurie had told him or what he'd realized about her.

She walked to the kitchen counter and picked up the property brochure. "A stay at the cottage comes with an opportunity to plant something on the farm. I think I read somewhere that at this time of the year, we'd be able to plant something in the garden."

As she continued talking and Mace shut the door, he couldn't stop himself from taking a good look at her. In the past, he'd witnessed Zurie with her walls up, and like many, including her only family, he'd viewed her at times as cold and unfeeling. But to be the person she'd needed to be to keep Tillbridge together all these years, she'd had to shut off her emotions to a certain extent. Because of that, she'd become fiercely independent, driven, and she'd developed some crazy belief that she couldn't have a life of her own and run Tillbridge. Theo leaving the way he had probably reinforced that in her. Without an outlet or someone she could count on to share her burdens with, it made sense she was stressed out.

But she wasn't alone. And she was wrong when she'd said that she wasn't enough for Tillbridge. She was more than enough, and she'd done enough. She just didn't see it. And knowing her, she wouldn't even hear him if he tried to tell her that. What she needed was for someone to show her and remind her on a daily basis that she deserved the same happiness that Tristan had found with Chloe and Rina had with Scott.

But he didn't have time. They had three more weeks together. Less than that when he factored in the days he'd be away in California. And even if he could convince her to agree to keep seeing him beyond the wedding, they'd only have a few more months.

Frustration and a weird sense of helplessness he couldn't define went with Mace as he walked over to Zurie.

She gave him a perplexed smile. "So is that look on your face a yes or a no on planting in the garden tomorrow?"

"If that's what you want." He brushed his lips over hers, planning to end it at that. They were going to have to get up early if they were going to the garden.

But one brief kiss wasn't nearly enough. He gave in to the need to hold her, to pull her against him. To hold her tighter as she wrapped her arms around him. She was more wonderful than any sip of wine he'd ever tasted.

As Mace backed her up toward the bed, brief stops allowed for the removal of shoes and clothing. Urgent kisses made up for the wait, and they intoxicated him. Soon all he could focus on was the softness of her lips and the lush warmth of her mouth. The silkiness of her skin gliding beneath his palms.

He followed her down on the mattress, anxious

to claim her mouth again. Need rose inside him as her passion matched his own. She arched up to meet his touch as he stroked over her breasts, down to her lower curves and between her thighs. He savored her moans and the breathy whisper of his name.

Moments later, sheathed in a condom, he entered her. She fit so perfectly around him, he lost a breath as she wrapped her legs low on his waist and he grasped on to her hips. Moving with her robbed him of thought and threatened to take away his sanity as his mind centered on one thing—pleasing her before he allowed himself to fall with her in that sweet place of release.

"What should we call him?" Zurie, kneeling in the dirt, wearing gardening gloves with yellow suns printed on them, held a foot-high tomato plant just plucked from the pot in her hands.

Midmorning on Sunday, they were the only ones in the greenhouse yards away from Summer House Lodge. The large, clear structure was filled with rows of tomato, pepper and strawberry plants and lettuce, peas and other greens along with flowers in pots on a shelf.

The earthy sweet and green scent of the plants that hung in the air was vented through an opening in the curved roof.

Mace took a knee beside her. The excited gleam

that had been in her eyes since she'd bounded out of bed that morning was still there.

He swiped a streak of dirt from the curve of her cheek with his bare fingers. "I have no idea what to name a plant. You choose."

She studied the plants. "I think he looks like an Ollie."

"Looks like an Ollie? Wouldn't that be a better name for an olive tree?"

"No." She sang out the word with a slightly affronted look. "Naming an olive tree Ollie would so cliché. That's the same as naming a tomato plant Tiberius or Thaxter."

"As opposed to Tom?"

Zurie gave him a hard stare. "You just don't get it." She looked to the plant. "But you do, don't you, Ollie?"

She was talking to a plant? Who was this woman? He liked her a lot. "So, what do we need to do to get Ollie into his new home?"

"First, you have to put on your gloves."

He slipped a match to her gloves, a gift from the farm, from his back pocket and put them on. "Okay, now what?"

Zurie ignored the small slip of instructions on the ground next to her and pointed. "I've already dug the hole."

She'd actually handled the garden tool with finesse when she'd done it. Something that had surprised him, considering how she'd wielded the cake spatula like a weapon at the tasting.

Maneuvering the plant carefully, she gently set it inside the space created for it. "Now I'm going to hold him upright while you fill in the hole."

He scooped up the dirt she'd dug out of the hole, and as he filled in the space around the plant, his shoulder bumped lightly against hers. "Like this?"

"Yes. But don't pack it in. It needs to be loose. The water will mold it to the soil and roots of the plants."

"You sound like you've done this before."

"We had a small garden at the back of the house until I was about, I don't know, ten or eleven, maybe? What about you? Have you ever planted anything?"

He took his hands away, allowing her to better arrange the soil. "My mom would plant flowers every spring. I reseeded my lawn at the house. Does that count?"

Smiling, she poured water on the soil from a watering can. "Your grass isn't dead, so yes." Setting the watering can aside, she gently laid straw underneath the plant then tore up the instructions and mixed the paper into the ground cover.

While Zurie surveyed her work, he surveyed her. She was beautiful like this, all lit up from the inside out.

She sat back on her heels and sighed. "It's up to you now, Ollie. I expect to see you with lots of tomatoes."

How could she see Ollie with lots of tomatoes? Maybe she'd visit on her own like he had, just to get away. Or maybe she'd bring someone else. A vision of her coming back with some faceless guy and enjoying the vineyard with him sprang into his mind.

Zurie nudged him. "Why are you scowling?"

"I'm not." He stripped off the gloves.

Making a conscious effort to relax the muscles in his face, he stood. As he held out his hand, she took it and he pulled her up to her feet and into his arms.

Mace pressed his lips to her forehead, which was warm from the temperature of greenhouse.

The sun was rising higher. Signaling the coming shift from morning to afternoon.

"Breakfast and then we hit the road?" *I wish we didn't have to leave...* That's what he wanted to say, but what was the point? They had to go back to Bolan...and pretend to be engaged.

"Yes. Breakfast first sounds good." From the dimming of the light of happiness in her eyes, Zurie felt the same way he did about their weekend coming to an end.

Chapter Twenty-One

Zurie turned off the 5:00 a.m. alarm on her phone. Responsibility warred with the part of her that wanted to stay in bed until seven or eight. It had been that way since she'd returned to work two days ago.

She sat up and slid her legs from under the sheets, but instead of rushing to stand up, she sat there with her eyes closed, just like the app Mace had downloaded on her phone the first morning and afternoon they'd spent together had taught her. She wasn't going to let those first fifteen minutes slip away from her. That's what she'd vowed two days ago, on Monday, when she'd made a promise to herself to make it habit. Along with the other changes she'd made.

Herbal tea still wasn't her favorite thing, but the rooibos blend that she was drinking as her current substitute for coffee was…tolerable. But the one habit she was still struggling with was not seeing Mace.

Three whole days had passed since they'd left the vineyard, and it felt like weeks since she'd seen him. He'd been working. She'd been catching up at her desk. They'd sent a couple of text messages to each other, but she'd refrained from sending more. She didn't want to appear too needy.

But the problem was that during her staycation, she'd had the freedom to see him whenever he wasn't working. Back then balancing her time and attention hadn't been an issue. Now it was, and in a big way.

The distraction of Mace, that's what she'd hoped to avoid by cutting things off with him when her staycation had ended. She still could, in a way. Couldn't she? Just because they were fake engaged didn't mean that they had to be together every day. And Mace working nights was the perfect explanation for spending so much time apart. They were on different schedules.

On the drive home from Sommersby, they'd also come up with a strategy to handle curiosity and keep hiding the truth. They would neither confirm nor deny that they were engaged. A grin from him, a coy smile from her, and Anna's rumor running amok would take care of it. They wouldn't have to really say or do anything to keep the ruse going.

So, there it was. She could wean herself off seeing him if that's what she wanted. But she didn't. She wanted more trips to the vineyard with him. More movies under the stars. More nights in his arms.

The reality of that sliced through her peacefulness, following her as she got ready for work. Everything suddenly felt off. The navy pantsuit she put on felt restrictive. The sensible black pumps she'd worn so many times in the past seemed too tight. Her schedule too full.

At eight o'clock, sitting at her desk in her office, she scrolled through the calendar on her desktop. A virtual meeting with Kayla at eight thirty. A meeting at nine with a company rep to look over a new point-of-sale system. And she needed to review and give input on the activity schedule and budget Tristan had drawn up for the new arena.

Meetings and tasks lined up one after the other on her schedule day after day all week. Just looking at it made her head spin. But it wasn't a lot. She used to thrive on every hour being filled. Was it just because of Mace? It couldn't be. Post-staycation blues… was that a thing?

Googling it... Not for staycations for definitely for vacations—same difference. Zurie pulled up the article. Reestablish sleep. *Check.* Use memories of your vacation to reduce stress. Ooh, she liked that one. Realize how much you enjoyed being out in the world and...*take a staycation*. Well, that advice wasn't helpful.

Her phone rang on her desk. She glanced at the screen. Hit ignore, that's what she should do. One more habit to build starting today. Don't talk to Mace every day. As if her hand had a mind of its own, she snatched up the phone and tapped the answer icon. "Hello."

"Good morning." Mace's low, laid-back tone signifying he was at the end of his day sent a rush through her more potent then caffeine.

"How did last night go at work?"

"Busier than usual, and not in a good way. But the calls I handled last night weren't the most interesting part of my shift."

"Oh? What was?"

"One of my colleagues pulling me aside to ask about the rumor he'd heard about me being engaged to you."

"And what did you say?"

Mace chucked. "I neither confirmed nor denied, just like we said. What about you? How's your morning going?"

"Good. Strange. Getting back into my schedule still feels...different. It's hard."

"That busy?"

"Yes and no. I miss you." The confession slipped out.

"You do, huh?" He chuckled softly. "In that case, you should probably open your door."

Mace strode down the mostly empty corridor past Pasture Lane, headed for Zurie's office. He'd planned to stick to text messages as their prime way of communicating for a few more days. That's what she seemed to want, and he didn't want to crowd her space.

But just now on the phone, it had sounded like she wanted to see him as much as he wanted to see her.

The door at the end of the hall opened, and Zurie stood in the threshold of her office, too tempting for him take his eyes off her.

He picked up the pace.

Security cameras high above in the corners were clocking his every move. He'd supervised their installation. But right then, he almost didn't care who was watching them on the monitors downstairs in the security room.

When he reached her, somehow, he managed to pull up enough restraint to wait until he was inside, and the door was shut behind him, before he kissed her.

Zurie's lips curled up in a smile against his. She slipped her arms around his neck as he held her by the waist. "You taste a little like coffee. Are you trying to torture me?"

He leaned away a little. "Sorry. No, that wasn't the plan."

"What exactly was the plan?"

"Holding and kissing you like I've been thinking about since I got off work." And like he'd been dreaming of every night since they left the vineyard.

She smiled up at him. "I like your plan."

"Speaking of plans, what's on your agenda for this week?"

"I still have work to catch up on, and Chloe, Rina and I have a dress fitting Thursday night. Why?"

Mace stepped back and reached into his front pocket. He'd never done what he was about to do with anyone before, but with Zurie, it felt right.

He slipped out his spare house key, took her hand and dropped it into her palm.

Her gaze moved from the key to his face. "Why do you want me to have this?"

Mace read wariness in her eyes and suddenly realized the confusion that was probably going through her mind. Giving the person you're seeing a key to your house was considered a big deal. *Damn.* He was doing it all wrong. He should have set it up better, not just put the key in her hand.

Smiling, he took hold of her other hand. "No pressure. I thought you should have it in case you wanted to stop by my place Friday night. I'll be at work, but there might be some wine and other special things in the refrigerator for you then. And if you did decide to drink the wine, you wouldn't be able to drive home afterward, so you'd have to sleep in my bed, which shouldn't be too much of hardship since it's much bigger than yours."

Relief opened up his chest as humor replaced the wariness in her eyes. She closed her hand around the key. "That's quite a plan."

"Oh, but there's more." He tugged her closer. "If you did decide to do all that, we could have breakfast when I got off work in the morning. And afterward, I don't know, all that cooking and eating could make you tired, and you might need a nap."

Zurie laughed as he laid his forehead to hers. "How long did it take for you to come up with this?"

"All of the hours I've been missing you since the vineyard." That admission should have bothered him. He should have been concerned about getting to this place in his head with Zurie so soon.

Maybe his feelings had gotten involved, like Tristan had predicted. But staying away from Zurie right now made less sense to Mace than being with her. He leaned back and looked into her eyes. "Say yes. Please."

Chapter Twenty-Two

Zurie climbed the steps to Rina's apartment carrying a large tote with the shoes and the shapewear she planned to wear with her bridesmaid dress. At nine thirty at night on Thursday, Main Street was mostly deserted. Just a couple of people walking their dogs and workers from the wine bar and shop heading to their cars parked on the opposite end of the street.

No one was paying attention, but as the wedding got closer, a part of her half expected someone to jump out of nowhere with a camera and a mic demanding to know what was going.

But so far, at least tonight was going as planned. Rina had gotten all three dresses upstairs in boxes without hitch, along with Charlotte's sewing machine in a rolling bag. Everything would go back out the same way, but the dresses would go to Rina's house for safekeeping until the day of the wedding.

Zurie knocked on the door.

Moments later, Rina opened it. They'd both had the same idea about clothes—leggings, T-shirts and ballet flats.

"Hey." Zurie paused to give Rina a hug before walking into the entryway.

"Hey, yourself, Miss Engaged Lady." From Rina's mischievous smile, she already knew it was a fake engagement.

"When did you find out about it and who told you?"

"Last Friday night. Darby was the first one to corner me about it. She'd heard it from a customer. I tried to call you, but you didn't answer, so I reached out to Tristan, and he told me everything. Including what happened with Chloe's ring. I can't imagine what those hours were like trying to find it."

"It was really hard on him. Luckily it turned up."

"I don't know if I'd classify Anna as lucky, but you're right. At least the ring was found."

They walked into the living room. The same table and chairs from the day of the tasting sat in the space. The ceiling lights reflected in the large tinted windows.

Just as Zurie was about to ask if Chloe was there,

Chloe's voice along with Charlotte's echoed through the apartment.

Zurie put her tote on the table and sat down.

Rina sat in the chair beside her. "So were you and Mace together before or after you spilled your iced coffee on him?"

That day seemed so far in the past. "After."

"So you spilling coffee on Mace wasn't just an unfortunate accident."

"Oh no." Zurie warned her off. "You are not going down the road of how me spilling coffee on Mace was similar to Scott running into you."

Rina shrugged with a smile. "Whatever you say. Once Chloe and Tristan are settled into their routine, we need to sync our schedules for a triple date night—me and Scott, Tristan and Chloe, and you and Mace."

Zurie hesitated.

"Why the face? Don't tell me you two aren't into date nights. It'll be fun."

"No, that's not it, but..." Saying it out loud felt so wrong but it was the truth. "Mace and I won't be together after the wedding."

"But why not?" Rina's face morphed from confusion to surprised realization. "You two are just hooking up until the wedding?"

Zurie didn't like the sound of that any more than what she'd admitted to Rina, but what Rina said was also the truth. "Yes, but that wasn't the original plan.

We were just supposed to be together over my staycation, but then the fake engagement extended things until the wedding."

Rina grinned and flipped her loose braids over her shoulder. "Look at you making the most of your time off. But why the limitations?"

"Trying to manage Tillbridge and balance a relationship is hard." Giving in to the need to unburden herself, Zurie added, "I can't focus. I'm fighting the distraction of Mace on my mind every day." And it was even worse since he'd given her the key to his place. She hadn't fully committed to spending Friday night at his place, but it was tempting.

"And you think that when you stop seeing him, that will magically disappear." Rina chuckled. "You're fooling yourself. It will probably get worse. The whole absence-makes-the-heart-grow-fonder thing is true. Trust me, I know. Why fight it? Especially since being with him is so good for you."

"Good for me? What do mean?"

"You look fabulous. And you're actually relaxed. You've been here ten whole minutes just talking to me and you haven't reached for your phone once."

Zurie's gaze drifted to her tote. That was true. She hadn't thought about her phone at all until Rina just mentioned it. And she was more relaxed and did have Mace to thank for that, but still… "Things are good between us now, but if we stayed together and things didn't work out, it could get awkward. He and

Tristan have been friends longer than Mace and I have been together. That wouldn't be fair to Tristan."

"I see your point. It could be risky." Rina reached over and squeezed her arm. "But what if it worked out?"

Zurie slipped the key into the lock and opened the door to Mace's house.

The alarm panel beeped, and she keyed in the visitor code that he'd given her to disarm the system.

The floor lamp in the corner of the living room automatically came on, illuminating the simply furnished space with a gray couch, wood coffee table, side tables and a large screen in a built-in cabinet situated between two gray and blue abstracts.

The ceiling light had also come on in the hallway to the left, leading to the main and guest bedrooms.

After closing and locking the door and putting the alarm on stay mode, she walked into the living room and dropped her purse and small blue overnight bag on the couch. She'd been to Mace's house plenty of times, but being there without him in the simply furnished space felt familiar and strange at the same time. Was she imagining it, or could she smell his woodsy cologne hovering in the air?

A text buzzed in on her phone, and she took it from her purse. Mace had mentioned that he would get a message on his phone alerting him that she'd gone inside.

You good?

Yes

Make yourself at home. Don't forget to check out what's in the refrigerator—bottom shelf. See you in the morning.

The morning seemed so far away. But she had work to keep her busy and the surprise Mace had left her in the fridge.

After slipping off her sandals by the couch, she went into the kitchen. She flipped on the wall switch, and light flooded the space. Just like the rest of the house, it was clean and neat with a plate and silverware on the drying rack by the sink.

She opened the refrigerator and peeked inside. An artfully arranged assortment of fresh grapes and dark chocolate–dipped pineapple, apple wedges and strawberries in a domed container sat on the bottom shelf along with a bottle of white wine from the Somersby vineyard.

Unable to resist, Zurie partially opened the plastic container, slipped out an apple wedge and took a bite. *Delicious.* The man just knew how to make her day.

A short time later, she'd changed into her favorite gray leggings and blue-striped crew-neck shirt with the sleeves pushed up. She settled on the couch with a glass of wine in her hand and some of the fruit on a small plate on the side table next to her.

Zurie took a sip of chardonnay, and contentment settled inside her. After talking to Rina last night during the dress fittings, she'd made up her mind about staying overnight at Mace's house...and broaching the topic of them staying together beyond the wedding.

The weeks they'd spent together had been really good so far. And their weekend at the vineyard had been nothing short of perfect. If anything, why not stay together for more of that?

More time together, that was probably something he'd be interested in, too, wouldn't he? When they'd first gotten together, he had settled for three weeks because that's what she'd insisted upon, not because that's what he wanted. Mace had told her to trust her instincts, and they were telling her that she and Mace were on the same page.

An hour or so later, content and pleasantly drowsy, she washed the plate and glass she'd used and went to the bedroom.

Mace's king-size bed with a tan comforter dominated the room.

After brushing her teeth and doing her facial cleansing routine, she started to crawl into bed. Her phone...she'd left it in the living room, and it needed to be recharged. The battery life was at less than thirty percent when she'd been texting with Mace.

Zurie went to her overnight bag, searching inside it for her charging cord. Wait. No. It was in her car. She was ready for bed and the house was locked up. She wasn't going outside now.

Make yourself at home. That's what he'd said in his text. And she really needed to charge her phone. He had spare cords. She'd used one before. He'd gotten it from his office.

Flipping lights on along the way, Zurie walked down the hall and into the bedroom he'd converted into a home office–slash–workout space. She walked past the weight bench and behind the desk on the far wall.

No cords on top. Shoot. Wait, no, there it was underneath some papers on the right. As Zurie slipped out the phone cord, the heading on a paper caught her eye.

State Bar Exam Nevada

She reached for the paper but then drew back her hand. She wasn't a snoop…but she needed to know. Zurie's stomach dropped as she sat in the desk chair to look through the stack of papers. He was working his way through an instructions list, and most of the items were there…along with one that had dates for the exam. The one that was six months from now was circled.

Mace was moving to Nevada. And it made perfect sense. Most of his family was there. He didn't have anyone in Bolan. At the vineyard, Mace had said he'd take the bar exam when the timing was right. And apparently, that was just a few months from now. When had he made the decision? Before or after their trip?

Zurie sat back in the chair, numbness setting in as she ran the evidence through her mind and faced reality. One, Mace didn't owe her any explanations about what he planned to do now or months from now. What they had was temporary. Two, she'd been through this before. Years ago, she'd known from the start that Theo was ambitious. But she'd foolishly believed that she'd come before his drive for success.

Mace had ambitions, too. He wanted to become a lawyer and practice in Nevada and be with his family. That was his priority. Not her or their relationship. And it was time for her to accept that… starting now.

Chapter Twenty-Three

"Raccoons? That's what all that noise was about? Are you sure?" The woman in her late seventies, standing in the brightly lit foyer of her home, stared skeptically at Mace. "It sounded like someone was breaking into the shed. They made such a ruckus."

"I understand, Mrs. Davies." He slipped his Maglite into the tactical belt around his waist. But I chased the raccoons out and made sure the shed was locked. They shouldn't bother you any more tonight."

"Well, good." Relief flooded her light tan face, framed by soft white curls, as she lifted a hand and clutched the collar of her light pink robe closed over her chest. "Thank you for coming out here. I always feel so much better when it's you."

A noise in the woods past the backyard of her older one-story house. A possible vicious dog on her property, a cat stranded in a tree. That was just the short list of reason why Etta Davies called the sheriff's department at least once every other week. Some of her calls required some sort of minor action. Many did not.

The habit of her calling and reporting suspicious activity around her home at night had started a year ago, after her husband had died. Some considered her a nuisance, but she was just lonely. It was an unspoken understanding that if she called in and Mace was on duty, he'd take care of her.

Mace reached for the doorknob. "Be sure to lock up behind me."

"Wait. I just baked some banana nut muffins. I'll get you some."

Before he could stop her, she'd hurried off.

It was a slow night. He could wait. If he didn't stay for this part of what had become a ritual, her feelings would be hurt.

A moment later, she returned with the muffins wrapped in foil and handed them to him. "Here you go. A half dozen should get you through the night."

"Thank you." He turned to leave.

"You know, years ago, I used to make my Joe a snack to take with him to Tillbridge..."

Mace turned, patiently listening to the account he'd heard more than few times about Mr. Davies, who had been a groundskeeper at Tillbridge.

Long minutes later, she patted his arm. "I'm glad you found Zurie Tillbridge. You're a good man, like my Joe. You deserve someone good to come home to."

Anna's rumor was traveling far and wide. "Thank you."

"When's the wedding going to be?"

Playing the confirm-or-deny game wouldn't work with Mrs. Davies. She'd just keep asking questions. "I don't know. I have to go now. You get some rest."

The end of his shift came later than expected. After finishing paperwork and changing into his street clothes, he skipped the usual catch-up time with the other deputies in the locker room and went straight to his truck and headed home.

At eight thirty on a Saturday morning, traffic was steady.

You deserve someone good to come home to...

When was the last time he had someone actually waiting for him to walk through the door? It had been so long he couldn't remember. Excitement moved through him as he thought of Zurie at his house. He couldn't wait to see her.

Mace pulled into his subdivision. A few turns later, he drove down his street and spotted Zurie's car in his driveway. His heart beat faster as he resisted breaking the speed limit. He parked behind her Mercedes in the driveway, jumped out and strode down the stone path leading to the front of his home.

Unlocking the door was suddenly a tedious task he couldn't get done fast enough. He opened it. Was that bacon he smelled? After shutting and locking the door behind him, he followed the wonderful smell of food to his kitchen and Zurie.

Mace paused, taking in the sight of her checking something in the oven. She'd already gotten dressed in jeans and a loose light purple top with thin shoulder straps. He'd hoped she'd stay awhile. Did she have someplace to go?

As she shut the oven door, she looked over at him. "Hi." Her smile curved up her lips, but it didn't flood her face with the happiness he'd expected to see.

"Good morning." He walked over to her, and as he went to embrace her, she laid her hands on his chest, subtly holding him back as she gave him an all-too-brief kiss, then slipped from his arms.

Prickles subtly danced along his nape. His internal warning system. Or maybe he was just reading her wrong.

"You had frozen waffles, so I made them. They're in the oven." She took plates down from the cabinet.

"Thank you for making breakfast. Was there something wrong with the toaster?" He pointed to the appliance in the corner to the right of the stove.

Zurie stared as if seeing it for the first time. "Oh, I missed it." She reached for the silverware drawer.

Unable to ignore the unease that now radiated into him, he took hold of her hands. "What's going on?"

"Going on? I'm making breakfast." Zurie gave him a smile that was even weaker than the one she'd given him when he'd first walked in.

He pulled her toward him then slid his hands up to gently grasp her arms. "You've used that toaster at least twice. What's wrong? Tell me."

She closed her eyes for a moment. And when she opened them, he saw the Zurie he used to know. The one who put up walls to keep people at a distance.

She released exhale. "I can't do this."

Dread and frustration tightened in his gut. "Do what?"

"This." As Zurie looked around, she lifted her arms slightly from her sides, gesturing to the kitchen and loosening hold. "Us."

She laid her hand lightly over his heart. In a minute, she'd feel it in her hands, because her words were carving it out of his chest.

Zurie looked up at him. "I loved the week we spent together during my staycation. I loved our getaway trip to the vineyard. But trying to be girlfriend and boyfriend for the long term, it's just not me. I love my job. It isn't so much that Tillbridge has to be the priority. I want it to be."

He looked into her eyes, searching for the lie, but all that was there was sincerity. She meant it.

Mace's heart twisted painfully in his chest as he let her go. "I understand. I get it."

Her priorities lay at Tillbridge and his lay in Reno. It was as simple as that.

Chapter Twenty-Four

Four long days. Ninety-six hours, and if she really thought about it, Zurie could break it down to minutes, maybe even seconds since she'd walked out of Mace's house and out of his life. And she'd used the breathing techniques she'd learned over her staycation to keep herself together while each word she'd told him had felt like a tiny paper cut opening in her chest.

Zurie sat back in the chair in her office, still feeling the hurt all the way into her bones. Along with the irony of it. Not lying to him had made it easier, too. It wasn't so much that Tillbridge had to be the priority. She wanted it to be. Loving Tillbridge was safer. It wouldn't break her heart.

A knock sounded at the door.

She clicked the camera icon on her desktop screen. A man she didn't recognize stood outside the office. Her door didn't have a sign on it. Someone must have directed him to where she was.

Zurie got up, smoothing down the front of her dress as she schooled helpful politeness on her face. She opened the door. "Hello, may I…"

No. It couldn't be. It wasn't him. She was conjuring him up in her mind. But it looked like him—right age, too, probably in his late thirties, except this guy had a shaved head instead of short hair. He wasn't clean shaven, but a close-cut beard and mustache shadowed his brown face. And he was wearing a button-down shirt and jeans instead of an impeccable designer suit and silk tie.

"Hello, Zurie."

But the voice was unmistakable.

Theo gave her a tentative smile as if he wasn't sure what to expect from her.

"Hi. This is…unexpected." They hadn't parted acrimoniously when they'd ended their engagement. She didn't hate him. She'd just never anticipated seeing him again.

"I hope you don't mind that I just showed up like this. I tried to call you last week, but your assistant said you were on vacation until this week. I'm passing through. I took a chance on catching you." He pointed back down the corridor. "Any chance you're free for coffee?"

"You came here to ask me out for coffee, right now?" The universe, fate, they were mocking her. That was the only answer for this.

"Yes, I am. This is probably going to sound funny to you." He chuckled as he looked down and scratched the back of his head. "But I'm here to talk to you about buying a horse."

As Zurie sat at her table in Pasture Lane, her mind wandered to Mace sitting in the chair where Theo now was. In weird way, it felt like cheating, but it wasn't. She and Mace weren't together. And Theo—even if she wasn't hurting right now, she'd never consider getting back with him. Hopefully he wouldn't go that route.

As Theo sipped from coffee from a cardboard cup, he glanced at the tea in hers with a slightly puzzled expression. No doubt he was remember how she lived for coffee.

A lot had changed in seven years. She was drinking tea, and he was interested in equines. "So, how's life in the investment world?"

"I wouldn't know. I gave it up about five years ago."

Wow. He must have really hit it big if he'd walked away from that life. "What do you do now?"

"I own a plant nursery in Dallas."

"Plant nursery—you mean like a tree or a flower farm?" Something massive, no doubt, with a good return.

"No. Just a plot of land next to a local flower shop."

"You own a flower shop and a plant nursery. That's…wonderful."

"It is." His serene smile pulled her in to look at him more closely.

When she'd dated him, he'd always been confident with a tiny trace of arrogance. By now he would have bragged a little bit about how big his flower shop was or how much money his plant nursery was making.

Puzzled, she asked. "So why do you want a horse?"

"For my wife as an anniversary present."

Zurie coughed down a sip of rooibos. When they'd broken up, he'd mentioned probably not considering marriage again until he was in his forties.

He clapped her on the back. "You okay?"

"Yes." Curiosity, too many unanswered questions—she had to know. "I'm sorry. What happened? You were on your way to the top of the investment world."

"I was." Theo smiled ruefully. "But then something unexpected happened."

"You met your wife?"

"That happened later. A year or so after I got to

Dallas, I was winning as an investment manager, but then I came down with pneumonia. I didn't know that at first. I was taking meds for the flu and working from home. I got worse. No one noticed or cared that I hadn't been in touch with anyone at the office for almost a week."

"No one noticed?"

"Nope." He sat back in the chair. "Someone from my cleaning service found me. I was lucky."

"That's horrible. Not that the cleaning service found you, but the rest." Surely if she didn't come down from her suite for a few days, Tristan or Rina would come looking for her.

But during end-of-year budget analysis, she was known for barricading herself in her suite for a couple of days with the threat of losing a vital body part for anyone who interrupted her until she was done. Not even Tristan or Rina dared to interrupt her. But Mace probably would. He'd make her open the door. Kiss her senseless. Then feed her and make her take a break. And if the tables were turned, she would do the same for him. Or at least she would have if…

She swiped the thought aside. "So, right after that, you quit your job."

"Pretty much. For a couple of years, I worked independently as a financial adviser. Bought a house. Really got into the landscaping part of things. Something about putting plants in the ground intrigued me more than numbers."

Ollie, thriving in the greenhouse under the sun, flashed into her mind. "Putting down roots, maybe?"

"Yeah, I think that's part of it."

She hadn't meant to say that out loud. As Zurie studied Theo, she let her mind roll back in time, envisioning what might have been if they'd stayed together. Two people driven by their careers, their obligations, trying to make a marriage work. It wasn't pretty.

That day at the vineyard, she'd told Mace that she'd known her and Theo's breakup was for the best. But saying that had always been a knee-jerk reaction to the hurt of coming in second in Theo's life. Yet seeing him now, so happy in his life, she actually believed it. They'd both ended up right where they belonged.

Chapter Twenty-Five

Mace walked outside onto the deck at his brother's house carrying a dish of vegetable kebabs that his sister-in-law Gia had given him.

Late-afternoon sun beamed down, but an awning covering a built-in grilling station, picnic table and deck chairs shadowed the space.

His khaki cargo shorts and a tan shirt would also keep him cool.

Efraín, similarly dressed to beat the heat of the outdoors and the grill, glanced over at Mace as he rearranged pieces of chicken on the rack. "I forgot we were doing those. Go ahead and stick them in the mini fridge."

Mace did as his brother asked, opening the fridge built into the end of the station closest to the beige brick two-story house. He sat down at the picnic table and picked up his bottle of beer. "Thanks for letting me jump on your laptop."

"No problem." Efraín snagged his own bottle from the table. "Were you able to check in for your flight okay?"

"Yep. I'm all set. Gia asked about taking me to the airport, but you don't have to. You already took days off to hang with me. I can take a Lyft to the airport." Mace took a sip of beer.

Coming to Reno after the five-day crisis negotiation seminar in Sacramento hadn't been the plan. But he'd had vacation days he'd needed to use, and it had been the right time to take them. And he'd needed to clear his head before seeing Zurie at Tristan and Chloe's wedding that coming weekend.

Efraín waved him off. "I got you. One of the perks of being your own boss is that you can take off pretty much whenever you want. You'll see."

"Yeah, I guess I will."

And maybe he would sooner rather than later. Moving to Reno in the next couple of months was something he was considering. He could work under Efraín, getting his feet wet with corporate law cases, while he studied to take the bar. The more he thought about it, the more he could see it as the motivation he needed to make those final steps to becoming a lawyer.

Sounds of an argument traveled from the lawn.

Emilia tackled Leo onto the grass, trying to wrestle the ball from him.

"Watch the grill." Efraín shoved the tongs into Mace's hand and hurried to his children. "Emilia… Leo…no. *Ven acá.*"

The four-year-old twins immediately stopped tussling, and the ball rolled away. Following instructions, they got up and went to their father. As Efraín leaned down and spoke quietly to them, the two hung their heads. A moment later, Emilia and Leo hugged each other. Emilia retrieved the ball and handed it to Leo.

A strange sense of awe and pride opened up in Mace. His older brother was a dad. And he was using the same tactics their parents had used to settle arguments between them when they were kids. What had their parents used to say?

You should be taking care of one another, not fighting each other.

Efraín returned to the deck. Shaking his head, he reached for his beer on the picnic table. "Those two."

Chuckling, Mace turned the chicken. "Kind of reminds me of us growing up and you causing trouble."

"Me?" A laugh shot out of Efraín. "You were the one always testing the waters and getting away with it."

"No, that was Andrea."

Efraín opened his mouth as if to object but then changed his mind. "You're right. She was always talking us into things. Why did we go along with it?"

"Because she had us wrapped around her finger."

"She did. Just like Emilia has Leo wrapped around hers." As his brother looked to the lawn at his kids, love filled his expression.

A strange longing opened up in Mace. "You really like being a dad, don't you?"

Efraín grinned. "I do. It's a hard job sometimes, but Gia and I keep each other sane." As he sipped his beer, he studied Mace. "What's that look about? Are you actually considering settling down and going halves on a kid with someone?"

No sat on the tip of Mace's tongue, but the vision of two children around the age of Emilia and Leo, two little replicas, the best of him and Zurie, rose in his mind. Sharing the responsibility of raising kids. He could easily envision them doing that together. But he and Zurie didn't want the same things. She cared about Tillbridge. Not him.

As the image went away, the loss of that possibility hurt like a punch. It pushed out an answer. "I was. Not now, but maybe someday. But I was wrong."

"Seriously?" His brother sat down at the table and turned down the volume of the music on his phone. "This is new. With who?"

Mace held on to the word dying to come out. This

was the type of conversation he would have had with Tristan. But he couldn't. And he needed to talk it out so he could hear himself say it was really over. "Zurie Tillbridge."

"Really?" Surprise came over Efraín's face. "I knew you had a crush on her in high school. So that actually progressed to something when you got back to Bolan?"

"It did. But we're not seeing each other anymore."

"What happened?

Mace turned the chicken. "I wanted more, and she didn't." Okay, there, he'd said it.

"Wait, more as in marriage?"

Gia breezed onto the deck carrying an empty glass dish for the chicken. "Who's getting married?"

"He is." Efraín pointed to Mace as he took the dish from her. "Or at least he was. She said no."

"She who?" Gia asked.

"Zurie Tillbridge," Efraín said. "He had a crush on her when he was in high school."

"A high school sweetheart?" Gia looked to Mace with a puzzled frown. "How come I've never heard of her before?"

"Because we weren't high school sweethearts." As Mace brushed sauce on the chicken, rising smoke amplified the feeling that he was the one being grilled. Good thing he didn't mention the fake engagement. "I only started seeing her a few weeks ago."

Efraín's brows shot up. "You were only dating a

few weeks and you wanted more with her? Possibly even kids?"

"I'm confused," Gia said. "Did you ask her to marry you or didn't you?"

Weariness over the conversation grew inside Mace. "It doesn't matter, because she doesn't want more."

"But—" Efraín interjected. "Did you actually ask her that question?"

Mace halted the conversation with a raised hand. "*Ya. Terminé de hablar de eso.*"

Efraín and Gia exchanged a look.

Mace set the tongs down on the shelf. He wasn't trying to be evasive, but he really was done talking about it. What was the point? He and Zurie weren't getting back together.

Just as he was about to tell them that, the doorbell rang and Efraín and Gia both went inside.

Moments later, two couples and two boys around the twins' age walked out on the deck with Efraín. The kids ran off to play with Emilia and Leo.

Introductions were made, and soon laughter and conversation took over the space. Relieved the focus had shifted, Mace joined in.

One of the women owned a software company. The other worked with Gia at the hospital. The husband of the woman who owned the software company was an attorney like Efraín. The other man,

Jake, was a real estate agent. During dinner, Mace talked to him about houses in the area.

Emilia cut the conversation short when she grabbed Mace's hand and pulled him to the yard to play a game the kids had made up. It combined chase, hide-and-go-seek, and soccer and the rules seemed to change every ten minutes.

Chapter Twenty-Six

Hours later, with covered paper plates laden with leftovers and sleepy kids in tow, the couples left for home.

While Gia gave Emilia and Leo baths and got them ready for bed, Mace helped Efraín clean up the kitchen and the deck.

Once they were done, they both plopped down in the padded deck chairs.

Efraín loosed a jaw-cracking yawn. “Thanks for helping out. It’s great to have people over, but it’s a lot of work, especially with the kids. Sometimes just watching them run around sucks the energy out of me.”

Mace glanced at his brother and smiled. "Or maybe you're just getting old."

"Go ahead and crack jokes." As he looked ahead, Efraín rested his head back on the chair. "Your day will come when you're chasing your own kids 24-7 instead for a few hours. When it does, I'll remind you of this conversation."

"I know you will."

Efraín glanced over at him. "You spent a lot of time talking to Jake about houses."

"Yeah. I figured I should get a jump on things if I'm going to move out here in the next couple of months."

"One minute we can't get you out of Bolan. Now you can't wait to leave."

"And changing my mind is a problem? I thought you were anxious for me to move here."

"Not if it isn't what you really want. What changed your mind? Was it Zurie?"

Mace couldn't lie to his brother or himself. "Yes." He let the need to talk overtake him, explaining everything that happened with him and Zurie from beginning to end to Efraín. "She's got this idea in her head that Tillbridge is all she needs. I did my best to show her. I think what Theo did to her is still driving her thinking. She's afraid to take a risk."

"I see your point, but look at it from her standpoint. The guy left her for his career. She probably needs reassurances before she takes a chance with someone where that same scenario is a possibility. Did you talk about how a long-distance relationship might work between the two of you so she could understand it was less risky?"

"No, because I didn't tell her I was moving here."

"Oh." Efraín remained silent.

"Oh, what?"

Efraín leaned in. "You're either really confused or you are lying to yourself. You went to law school. Line up the facts. You said you wanted more with her. You didn't tell her you were planning to move here, and you've been stalling on taking the bar. The answer is clear as glass. As least it is to me."

Mace considered what Efraín was suggesting and he couldn't lie. "I admit. I wasn't sure if I was ready to take the bar yet. Not from a studying-for-it standpoint. Just life. But I felt that way before I met Zurie. As far as not telling her, I guess I didn't want to put that out there if I didn't have to because she was already putting limitations on our relationship. It was frustrating. There was nothing I could do to change her mind."

"Sometimes it's not about doing something. It's about being."

His brother sounded like a self-help manual. "It's more complicated than that."

"It's complicated because when you're used to making things happen, not doing anything to fix a situation doesn't compute for you. I get it. Do you remember when Gia and I were first trying to get pregnant?"

"Yeah, I remember it being a tough time for the two of you."

"It was. For me, one of the hardest parts of the process was seeing all that Gia had to go through physically and mentally. She's strong and tough, but even the strongest, toughest people in the world need a break, and I couldn't help lighten the load or reduce the expectations that she was putting on herself. Between the hormones and the disappointment month after month, she struggled, and at one point, she felt not being able to have children was a deal breaker for our relationship. Of course it wasn't. Even though I told her that, she started walling herself off from me. I could sense it, and there was nothing I could say or do to stop her."

The memory of Zurie telling him she couldn't continue their relationship came to his mind. In that moment, he'd felt that there was nothing he could say or do to stop Zurie from walking away.

Efraín continued, "One night, Gia and I got into a really bad argument. A lot was said, and I almost left. But before I walked out the door, I glanced back at her face, and I saw this look of acceptance as if she were telling herself, 'See? I was right. I knew he would leave.' And it pissed me off."

"What did you do?"

"I didn't leave. I told her that having children

might have been a question mark in our lives, but me loving her wasn't. No matter how hard she tried to push me away, I was going to be there for the rest of that day, and every day after that, because I loved her, and she needed to deal with it."

"And that solved everything?"

"Well, that, and what happened after I kissed her." Efraín grinned. "Close to eight months later, the twins were born." His smile sobered as he reached over and thumped Mace on the arm. "If Zurie means something to you, don't give up on her so easily."

"You realize if I go that route and try to get her back, I can't do it from here."

"Yeah, I know." Efraín released a slow breath. "Will I be disappointed if you don't move here and help run the firm? Yes. But if you're happy where you have a chance to build a life with someone you care about, I'll get over it. I just want you to be happy."

As Mace's plane lifted off from Reno-Tahoe International Airport, he closed his eyes, exhausted from lack of sleep. Last night, so many things had occupied his mind. They still did. His conversation with Efraín about Zurie. Mrs. Davies's life story with her husband. Zurie's question at the vineyard about if he felt behind in the relationship department.

Maybe he was behind when it came to relationships. He'd never committed to anyone fully. Not even Zurie. His brother was right. He hadn't been straight up with Zurie about Reno or how he felt about her. He'd given her no reassurance about him or their relationship. Instead he'd left room for doubt. And the more he thought about it, he may have instigated it that night she'd stayed alone in his house.

After she'd left that morning, he'd needed to charge his phone, and he'd looked for the cord he'd last used in his office. He'd been so frustrated about not being able to find it and Zurie leaving, he'd batted papers from his desk. He'd later found a charging cord neatly looped in a circle on his nightstand. He hadn't done that. When she'd gotten that cord from his desk, what else had she found? The Nevada bar exam checklist sitting right there on his desk?

Efraín was right—he hadn't been lining up the facts. If he had, he could have fixed it and made better decisions. When he reached his seventies, like Mrs. Davies, he wanted to look back on his life with happiness like her, not regret because he hadn't stopped long enough to share his life with someone. Funny. He'd always thought in terms of connection—that he and the right person would fit together, but maybe that wasn't what it was about at all. During his long weekend with Zurie, he'd shared a part himself with her. He'd also shared what he enjoyed, and she'd enjoyed it with him. And it had felt good to do that with someone. No. Not just someone. Zurie.

Seven hours later, Mace's flight landed in New York. His connecting flight wasn't for hours. Duffel bag on his shoulder, he walked through the terminal, not searching for his gate but for one that had the fewest number of people around.

He found a suitable space, dropped his bag in a chair by the window and took out his phone. He dialed the familiar number. His father picked up.

Mace took a breath and entered into the most difficult conversation of his life.

Chapter Twenty-Seven

Zurie glanced out the living room window.

At seven in the morning, instead of a clear blue early-morning sky, it was still as dark as predawn with various shades of light blue to gray providing a backdrop for the clouds.

A forty percent chance of rain later that morning was the forecast, but it looked more like eighty.

Should the wedding stay at the pavilion or should they move it to Pasture Lane Restaurant? An outdoor wedding with a view of the pasture and the hills was what Chloe and Tristan had wanted. Everything was still in place to make that happen. Switching to Pasture Lane would require changes that would need to start happening in the next hour or so to still pull the wedding ceremony off at one that afternoon. But what if she suggested moving the ceremony to the restaurant, and the weather morphed from rain into the perfect sunny day? She would be responsible for robbing them of the picturesque moment. But if she didn't urge them to make the change and the dark clouds forming in the distance delivered what they promised…

Images flitted through her mind of Chloe in her beautiful wedding dress and Tristan in his tux, huddled under the pavilion, or one of the tents with their guests, trying to escape the rain as puddles of mud rose higher and higher in the grass around them.

Anxiety curled into knots in her stomach. Zurie looked to the rooibos tea in her cup. She just couldn't drink it today. It wasn't satisfying her. She dumped it in the sink, praying that, unlike the tea, the wedding wasn't headed down the drain as well. Of all days, this was not the one for a downpour. Or to not have an objective sounding board. She missed Mace.

A longing for him blanketed her worry in something that made her want to scream. Sadness. She'd never been one to feel sorry for herself. She'd never had time for it in the past, and she didn't have time for it now. She and Mace were over. She'd broken up with him because it was the necessary thing to do.

Tristan and Chloe were taking an important step forward. Being their wedding planner was just like being in charge of Tillbridge—she had to let go of what was unimportant and keep her focus on what mattered. And keep her personal feelings out of it. This wedding had to be a beautiful memory Tristan and Chloe would cherish, rain or shine.

Just as she was about to pick up her phone from the counter, it rang. Tristan's name flashed on the screen. Perfect timing. He'd spent the night in the cottage he still owned on the property instead of his house. Chloe was staying with her family in a two-bedroom suite downstairs.

At the cottage, he actually had a better view of the south pasture than she did. Maybe by some miracle things looked hopeful from his point of view.

Zurie answered her phone. "Good morning."

"Good morning. So I'm sure you've been monitoring the weather. Chloe and I have been texting each other about it all morning. We keep going back and forth on the decision. What do you think we should do? Take a chance on staying in the pasture or go with the indoor plan?"

The window was closing on being able to set up Pasture Lane on time for the wedding.

What's your gut telling you?

The question Mace would have probably asked her hovered. She wanted the best for Tristan and Chloe, and she couldn't guarantee that with the weather working against them. Still, it was a tough call.

Zurie took one last look outside her living room

window, hoping to see a ray of hope, but only larger, darker, more ominous clouds existed. "I don't think we should risk it. Let's move the ceremony to Pasture Lane."

"Okay, then." He blew out an exhale. "Being able to see the hill where I proposed to Chloe while we took our vows, she was looking forward to that. I just hope she's not too disappointed."

It wasn't just Chloe who'd been looking forward to it. Tristan had, too. "She's marrying you. How could she be anything but happy today?"

He chuckled. "Thanks for saying that. I feel the same way about her, too."

"This is only one little hiccup. We'll get through it."

"Actually, there's two. Mace isn't back in Maryland yet. He called me last night. The same thunderstorm that's coming our way hit New York yesterday. His connecting flight from there to Baltimore was delayed, then canceled."

Mace had called Tristan instead of her. That made sense. They hadn't spoken to each other since she'd broken things off with him at his house. And burned the waffles. Smoke rising from the oven had capped off one of the worst moments in her life. He hadn't wanted her help in cleaning up the mess, so she'd left. And cried all the way home.

Stop. *Focus on what's important.* Remember? "Is

there a chance he'll be able to fly out this morning? It's a short flight."

"That was the plan, but his early-morning flight had a mechanical issue. He's having problems getting rebooked again. And they're still dealing with storms. He's going to try and rent a car."

But road conditions probably weren't that great, either. He'd be driving into the storm. Concern for Mace's safety started to well inside her, and she tamped it down. As a sheriff's deputy, he knew the risks of driving in inclement weather. If it wasn't safe, he'd stay off the road.

But there was still one more issue with Mace and the wedding that had to be addressed. "Did he say anything about security for the ceremony?"

"He did. It's taken care of. His friend Dean is in charge. And as far as best man, Thad will take his place."

Crappy weather was one thing. Not having his best friend at his side as his best man because of it—that wasn't fair. "I'm sorry."

"It's not your fault. The weather is to blame."

But maybe Mace not being there *was* her fault. Guilt pinged. His original plans hadn't involved him being gone this long. "Is there anything I can do?"

"Check on Chloe for me?"

"I will. Once I get everything arranged in Pasture Lane. I'll text you what time to be downstairs. You remember the contingency plan entrance, right?"

"The loading dock. Tell me the time and I'll be there."

Zurie said goodbye to Tristan. As she slipped on her tennis shoes at the door, she went through a revised mental checklist for the day. *Yikes.* The minister. She'd almost forgot about calling him. And then she needed to text Rina about the change. And get in touch with Blake to make sure the tents were taken down at the pavilion before the rain.

Downstairs, after making those two important calls, she met up with Philippa in the dining room.

It had already been set up for the reception with the DJ in the far corner along with a portable dance floor.

Floral centerpieces with candles were already on the white linen–covered tables. Fanned beige napkins plus silverware were also set up. And now everything had to be shifted around.

Zurie gave Philippa an empathetic glance. "Everything looks beautiful. You and the staff did a wonderful job setting this up. I'm sorry we have to move everything around."

"Thank you." Philippa shrugged. "The tables will get a little messed up moving them back and forth. We'll just have to herd everyone out into the corridor immediately after the ceremony so we can put everything back in place. What about the kitchen and dining staff? Are we keeping them in the dark still about this being Tristan and Chloe's wedding ceremony until the last minute?"

"Once they see the tables lined up along the sides and chairs lined up forming a center aisle, they'll probably guess it's a wedding. But they still won't know who. Maybe hold off until a half hour before the ceremony? Don't forget to give them the cell phone talk."

"Oh, I definitely won't forget that."

No pictures of the wedding and no posting of info about the wedding on social media until after the reception was over was the courtesy they were asking from everyone, including the guests in attendance.

With the help of a few of the service staff, they rearranged the tables and chairs. Two tall ferns in brass pots were spaced out up front in the center of the room. Tristan, Chloe and the minister would stand between them.

All that was left was rolling out the white runner down the middle. But that wouldn't happen until the start of the ceremony. That way it wouldn't get dirty before Chloe walked on it.

Last stop was the suite where Chloe and her family were staying.

Zurie knocked on the door.

A more mature version of Chloe answered the door. The sleeves of Patrice Daniels's peach dressing gown billowed as she welcomed Zurie inside the suite and gave her a hug. "How's everything downstairs?"

"We're ready," Zurie replied. "How's everything here?" She allowed herself a moment to soak in the embrace.

Patrice gave the best hugs. Long and comforting with a nice tight squeeze before she let go. "We just finished a light breakfast. Have you eaten today, or have you been too busy running around?"

Zurie's stomach answered for her with a low growl.

Patrice, a dietitian, gave her an admonishing maternal look. "You'll have a muffin and some fruit before you leave. We can't have you passing out in the middle of the ceremony."

"Yes, ma'am." Feeling properly scolded, in a good way, Zurie followed her into blue-carpeted living area.

Chloe's father, Dr. John Daniels, a balding medium brown-skinned man with glasses, sat on the tan couch drinking coffee and talking on his phone. The cardiologist was already dressed for the wedding in dark slacks, a crisp white shirt and a blue tie.

He mouthed "good morning" to Zurie as she followed Patrice into small kitchen alcove adjoining the living room, where a catered continental breakfast of muffins, fruit, coffee, juice, water and packages of oatmeal were laid out on a wood table along with small plates, paper napkins, glasses and flatware.

Patrice picked up a small plate, put a banana muffin and grapes on it, and handed it to Zurie. "Start with that." She gestured for Zurie to have a seat at the table.

Zurie complied and munched a grape. "Thank you. Where's Chloe?"

"In the bedroom, getting ready and texting Tristan." Patrice chuckled and shook her head. "You'd think they hadn't communicated with each other in months. Once they're married, they'll have their whole lives to talk to each other. Even when they don't want to."

Patrice's dignified eye roll made Zurie laugh as she broke apart the muffin and ate a small piece. "I'm not surprised they're texting each other. They've been like twins, joined at the hip for months now. They even almost dress alike."

"I thought it was just me noticing that."

"Noticing what?" Chloe breezed in wearing a white robe. She kissed Zurie on the cheek then poured a glass of water from the pitcher on the table. Even with makeup, her complexion was dewy with a natural glow. Her curly hair was pinned into an updo.

"Nothing important." Patrice eyed Chloe's glass of water. "Make sure you ease up on the fluids before the ceremony. Nerves have a way of sneaking up on you once you're zipped into a gown. The last thing you want is to have to visit the ladies' room in your wedding dress, or worse..."

"Yes, Mom." As Chloe slipped into a chair at the table, a slight dimple appeared in her cheek with her small smile. "I will avoid having to make a pit stop right before the ceremony at all costs."

Zurie absorbed positive mother-daughter banter and loving energy swirling around her. Her mom would have gotten along with Patrice and adored Chloe. And Uncle Jacob would have spoiled Chloe. A pang of bittersweetness hit. The way Tristan looked after Chloe with such care and love, she saw glimpses of Jacob in him.

After dutifully finishing every bite of food on her plate under Patrice's watchful eye, Zurie rose from the chair. "I need to check on a few things before I head upstairs. Call if you need anything."

"Oh." Chloe laid her hand on Zurie's arm. "Two things you should know. Anna Ashford, the town journalist, cornered me yesterday, wondering if her invite to Tristan's party was lost in the mail."

"*Journalist* is a loose term when it comes to Anna. I definitely didn't send her an invite."

"Well…" Chloe gave a slightly sheepish look. "I added her to the guest list. I know she's a pain, but from my experience, it's better to win someone like her over with a bit of honey than waste time and money trying to get rid of them with repellant."

Chloe could have a point. "If you're comfortable having her here, then I am, too. What's the other thing?"

"My agent and publicist insisted on hiring a photographer. It's sort of a wedding gift–slash–make-sure-we-get-the-right-photos-for-publicity thing. Tristan already gave his name to security. Any word on Mace?"

"No. I haven't heard anything." Zurie tossed her paper napkin in the trash and put her plate in the sink with the rest of the dirty dishes. She'd have to get used to the "where's Mace" question, since many people thought they were engaged.

Chloe stood. "I hope he makes it."

Zurie did, too…for Tristan's sake, of course, not hers.

Chapter Twenty-Eight

Zurie faced the twenty-five guests standing in the seating area where the host podium was located, separated by a wall from the dining room of Pasture Lane Restaurant. Friends of Tristan and Chloe were attired in afternoon cocktail to dressy casual clothing.

She took a breath, trying to calm the butterflies in her stomach. Once she'd slipped on the chiffon dress with the high-low hemline and a blue-and-peach floral pattern, the feeling had erupted. This was it. In less than twenty minutes, the ceremony would start.

Flagging everyone's attention, she raised her voice over the crowd's conversations. "Hello, everyone.

Thank you for being here today for Tristan's surprise early birthday party."

Cora, a thin, birdlike older woman, waved her hand. "The invitation mentioned Chloe Daniels. Is she here?"

Cora's husband, Wes, a thin older man with a smooth bald head and a deep brown face, who was also the stable's farrier, gave her nudge trying to shush her.

"Good question." Anna Ashford joined in. "I believe I'm supposed to have an exclusive interview with her today."

Zurie had to stifle a derisive snort. Honey versus bug repellant. That's what Chloe had said, so she had to stick to the script. "There are actually a few surprises happening today. But I'm afraid that you're going to be the ones surprised…in a wonderful way."

Varying levels of confusion, doubt and wonder crossed the guests' faces. Anna and Cora leaned in with most eager expressions of all.

"Instead of celebrating Tristan's birthday…you're here because Tristan and Chloe wanted you to witness their vows and celebrate their union. Welcome to Tristan and Chloe's wedding ceremony."

Exclamations of surprise rose from the guests along with applause.

Zurie smiled along with them. "I know. Isn't it wonderful? And to keep it that way, we need to ask a huge favor." She have Anna a direct look. "Please don't text anyone that you're here right now or take photos or post about this affair on social media. Allow Tristan and Chloe a chance to have their day. There'll be plenty of time to share the good news tomorrow."

Many of the guests nodded in agreement. Anna dropped her phone back in her purse.

"In the dining room, we've lined up chairs along the aisle. Please sit there instead of at the tables. All right, then. Follow me."

Inside the dining room, the floral centerpieces with candles were lit. Combined with the natural light coming through the windows and the view of the gray-blue sky and intermittent rays of light peeping through the clouds, the space had an ethereal glow.

Slow love ballads, played by the DJ in the far corner, came through the speakers situated near the small dance floor.

Once the guests were seated, Zurie nodded to Philippa, who peeked into the kitchen.

A moment later the minister came out through the swinging door in a dark suit.

Tristan walked behind him.

Charlotte's instincts about the style of suit had been right. He looked beyond handsome in an impeccably tailored cream-colored tux paired with a white shirt and navy satin vest, tie and pocket square.

Instead of Thad... Mace walked out behind him.

Zurie's legs grew weak. *He made it.* Tristan must be so relieved.

GQ-worthy from head to toe in a navy suit with a white shirt, cream vest and tie, he stood near the ferns with Tristan and the minister.

Tristan looked solemn and a bit nervous as he adjusted the cuff links in his sleeves.

Mace clapped Tristan lightly on the back as if to let Tristan know he was there for him.

Tristan smiled and nodded.

Zurie tore her gaze away from Mace and sent a text to Rina that it was time for Chloe to arrive. Instead of coming through the lobby, Rina, Chloe and her parents were coming the back way to the corridor.

As she hurried out of the restaurant, she gave Blake a nod.

The trainer, who looked like a slightly older Bradley Cooper, had worn a dark suit for the occasion. With Scott's help, he would roll the white runners down the center aisle.

In the corridor, buffet tables had been set up on the right for the heavy hors d'oeuvres Philippa would serve after the ceremony. On the left, farther down, were two portable bars.

Two of the security detail Mace had organized stood on each end of the hall in dark suits. According to the plan Mace had sent her before they'd broken up, more security guarded the front door and were patrolling the grounds.

Coming from the direction of her office, Zurie spotted Chloe with a cream cape covering her dress and wearing a delicate floral tiara. Charlotte, in a tangerine dress, walked beside her.

John, now fully dressed in his dark suit, walked with Patrice, who'd put on a sky-blue dress and had styled her hair in messy bun that complemented her delicate features. Thad, a taller, leaner version of his father, with short, neatly clipped hair, walked with them. He wore the same suit ensemble as Mace.

Rina also walked with them, carrying the calla lily bouquets.

As they got closer. Chloe gave Zurie a huge, tremulous smile as she smoothed a tendril of hair from her cheek.

Charlotte untied the cape and slipped it from Chloe's shoulders. Chloe looked even more stunning then she had that day at Rina's house when she'd tried on the strapless mermaid-style dress with appliqués, beads, lace and a chapel-length train.

Zurie squeezed Chloe's hand. "You look beautiful. Are you ready?"

"Yes." Chloe squeezed back before accepting a pink calla lily bouquet from Rina.

Rina held out one of the two single white calla lilies in her hand to Zurie.

"Why are you giving this to me?" Zurie asked.

"You're walking down the aisle as a bridesmaid, too, since you don't have to run around anymore. Thad's standing up front with Mace and Tristan."

"I'll hold on to this for you. And don't worry, I'll take care of Chloe." Charlotte slipped the phone from Zurie's hand.

There was no time to argue.

Like clockwork, as Zurie had planned, Thad escorted his mom down the aisle to her seat.

Rina walked down next, and then it was Zurie's turn.

As she walked down the aisle, a million details swarmed in her mind. *I shouldn't be doing this. I need to make sure everything is ready for the reception.* Halfway down she met Mace's gaze, and every thought dissipated. Her heart swelled with happiness in seeing him there and hurt for the loss of him in her life at the same time.

Before she took her place, she looked to Tristan. Flooded with genuine happiness, she smiled at him and he smiled back.

The DJ cued up a classical string quartet version of the bridal chorus.

Head high and smiling, Chloe walked regally down the aisle on her father's arm.

Zurie caught a glimpse of Tristan. Stunned, captivated, happy—seeing his face as Chloe walked toward him brought tears to Zurie's eyes, and she blinked them back.

Chloe's and Tristan's gazes remained locked on each other, breaking away only when Chloe's father hugged her and then Tristan.

Chloe gave Zurie her bouquet, then turned back to Tristan.

Clearly in love with each other, Tristan and Chloe faced the minister.

...to have and to hold from this day forward, for better, for worse, for richer, for poorer, in sickness and in health, to love and to cherish, till death do us part...

The solemn, reverent words seem to hover in the air like a blessing.

Rings were exchanged, and a short time later, Zurie handed Chloe her flowers.

Now husband and wife, Chloe and Tristan walked back down the aisle.

And then it was Zurie's turn to walk with Mace. She looked into his eyes, and suddenly it felt as if her high heels were bolted to the floor.

Rina's subtle elbow nudge propelled Zurie to take one step and then another until she reached him.

She looped her hand through the crook of his arm. His strength, the weight of his hand resting lightly on hers, the cologne wafting from him. They all hit her at once. It was like being caught in a sudden downpour without a raincoat or an umbrella. She looked straight ahead, training her eyes on the end of the runner. That's when she could let go. What if she couldn't? What if she kept holding on to him like a part of her so desperately wanted to do?

A few steps before she should have, Zurie slipped her hand from his arm.

She joined Tristan and Chloe in the corridor. The two emanated pure joy as she hugged them both. "Congratulations."

"You did it!" Rina came over and gave the couple hugs and kisses.

"This way, please." A thin, silver-haired man with a camera waved them down the hall.

Chloe picked up the skirt of her dress. "We should go now before the guests start coming out, otherwise we won't be able to break away."

"Go on." Zurie nudged them forward. "I'll wrangle the guests and catch up with you in a minute."

"Security has it handled." Mace walked over to her. "They'll keep the guests in the corridor while we take pictures."

"Oh. All right." He stared down at her, and, once again, she suddenly found it hard to move. His scent—a mix of cologne and how it warmed on his skin—made her heady.

Guests filed out of the Pasture Lane, and as promised a blond member of the security team directed people toward bars and buffets with appetizers.

"We should catch up with everyone." Mace laid his hand on her back to guide her.

A spark of attraction and familiarity struck, but

icy reality replaced it, prompting her to walk faster and get away from his touch. They weren't together anymore. She had pull herself together. She couldn't fall apart or turn into a puddle every time he looked at her.

The photographer took candid and posed photos of Chloe and Tristan and the entire bridal party in the lobby and on the porch.

Staff members who'd just found out about what happened came to the lobby to see what was going on and to congratulate the couple.

Tristan and Chloe relaxed the no-photo rule to take a few pictures with the staff.

He called out, "Hey, guys, do us a favor and don't text or post them until we're gone, okay?"

Before Zurie's eyes, Tristan slipped into the role of celebrity husband, giving Chloe space to interact with her admirers, not taking offense when they didn't want him in a photo.

The hired photographer wrapped up taking photos of them.

Using the excuse of holding Chloe's train, Zurie avoided being near Mace and lessening the pull of proximity.

It was going to be a long afternoon.

Chapter Twenty-Nine

Food, dancing, conversation, laughter—it all flowed freely at the reception, along with the wine.

At the table during dinner, Zurie sat next to Chloe's father. He took a sip of the full-bodied red wine and nodded approvingly. "This is from a local vineyard?"

"Yes, it's just three hours away." As Zurie shared details about Sommersby, she relived a few of the moments from her trip there with Mace.

John staring at her alerted Zurie to the fact that she'd been talking nonstop.

She reached for her phone. "I have the info. I can airdrop it to you if you're interested."

"Please." He took his phone from his inside jacket pocket, and she sent him the info.

"Thank you." He slipped his phone back into his jacket. "What you described sounds like a great day trip to take before we leave. Next time we're in the area, we'll have to plan an overnight stay there. No offense to Tillbridge."

"None taken. It's a wonderful place. If you stay in the cottage, before you leave, you can plant something on the property and..." *Stop talking. You're boring the poor man.* Zurie shook her head. "I'm sorry. I'm rambling." She laughed. "Maybe it's because of the wine."

John gave her an indulgent smile. "Or you just enjoyed a memorable trip there with someone you care about. I understand. Patrice and I have experienced some great trips together. Special places, like the vineyard you mentioned, are our most unforgettable getaways. If you want my advice—keep doing them together. That's what's kept us together for thirty-five years."

Zurie pulled up a smile and nodded. Mace walking out the restaurant with Tristan caught her eye. There wouldn't be any more vineyard trips for them. Only memories carefully stored like a precious vintage in her mind.

At the bar in the corridor, Mace, Tristan, Thad and Luke, one of Tristan's bull-riding friends, raised shots of whiskey in a toast.

"Here's to Tristan," Luke said. As the dark-haired man, who looked more like a surfer than a bull rider, raised his glass a bit higher, he flashed a grin. "May his marriage to Chloe be a lot more successful than his bull rides."

Tristan laughed. "Okay. Don't make me go on YouTube and pull up some footage on you."

"Seriously, though." Luke's expression sobered. "I'm happy to see you this happy. And I wish you all the best in the years to come. To Tristan and Chloe."

Mace and Thad echoed the toast, and all four of them clinked their glasses before drinking the shot.

More toasts were made to Tristan before Thad and Luke returned to the dining room, leaving Mace and Tristan behind.

Tristan glanced over at Mace. "I know the drive wasn't easy in the storm. Thanks for making it today."

"Couldn't miss it."

Tristan stared down at the platinum wedding band on his hand. He shook his head. "On some level, this feels unreal. She married me."

Tristan's love-struck grin pulled a chuckle out of Mace. "If it helps, I can't believe she married you, either. If you want to keep her, my advice to you is burn all the photos of you as a kid wearing Superman pj's and a red towel as a cape. All that bull-rider street cred you have, gone. Don't do it."

"Oh, man. Who showed you those? Rina?"

"No. Actually, I haven't seen them. Zurie happened to mention it. She told me not to tell you I knew, but..." Mace shrugged. "Hey, I just couldn't let it pass."

Tristan chuckled. "Of course you couldn't." He studied Mace. "You and Zurie have been avoiding each other all afternoon. Is everything good between you two?"

Mace signaled to the bartender for two more shots. As far as avoiding, he wasn't. That was all Zurie. "Not as good as I'd like it to be. Remember when I told you that if I had a chance to spend time with the woman I want, I would, and then I told you it wasn't Zurie?"

"Yeah, I do." Tristan propped his elbow on the bar. "But let me guess, now she is."

"Right."

Tristan gave him an empathetic look. "Anything I can do? Do you want me to talk to her?"

"No." Mace took a drink from his glass. "This is something Zurie and I have to settle on our own."

Bubbles floated into the sunny sky along with the well-wishes and cheers as Tristan and Chloe hurried to the waiting black limo. As it pulled away from the curb and out of the parking lot, they waved goodbye and Chloe blew kisses out of the open window.

The crowd dispersed. Some went to their cars in the parking lot, while others went back inside the guesthouse. Standing off to the side of the entrance on the porch, Zurie gave in to fatigue and leaned her shoulder on Rina's, who stood beside her, still radiating energy.

Rina, scrolling through photos on her phone, released a happy sigh. "Oh, look at them. They look so wonderful." She held up her phone so Zurie could see the montage.

Somehow, Rina had managed to be everywhere at once, capturing candid, lovely, cute and humorous photos of Tristan and Chloe during the reception.

Rina paused on a photo of the two of them with Chloe in the suite after she'd changed into the cute pale blue midthigh dress she'd worn for travel to her and Tristan's mystery honeymoon destination. Chloe had given Zurie and Rina pale gray Stetsons with a personalized leather hat band with their name. Tristan had given the same with a different design to Mace and Thad, and she had pictures of that moment, too. They all looked good, but Mace held her attention.

Rina kept scrolling and slowed on photos of Mace and Zurie when Tristan had humorously shared that Zurie and Mace weren't really engaged.

The picture of Anna's sour-looking expression was priceless.

But one photo, of Zurie and Mace, pricked Zurie's heart. She and Mace were both faking a laugh in the photo. Pretending everything was okay. Could it get any worse? Actually, it could. They had pretended to be engaged, and now she had to pretend that everything was okay when she was around him…until he left in a few months. It hurt too much to think about it.

Zurie looked away from the picture. "I'm going upstairs to change. I'll be back down to help Philippa with cleanup." She turned to go through the door and smacked into a human wall.

As she faltered, Mace lightly grasped her arm. "Careful."

Zurie stared up at him. Seconds passed before she realized her hand rested on his chest. "Sorry." She went to move away.

He held on to her with one hand. The hat Tristan had given him was in the other. "Do you have a minute?"

"I should really go ch—"

"Sure, she does," Rina interjected, looking pointedly at Zurie as she walked inside. "I'll help Philippa."

If only Rina knew her matchmaking was in vain. Zurie pulled up a smile. "Well, I guess I do have a minute."

People scooted past them.

Mace let her go. "Can we go somewhere private? Like your office?"

"Sure." Zurie led the way inside the guesthouse.

As they walked side by side down the corridor, staff members folded up the buffet tables.

Once inside her office, Zurie shut the door behind her and Mace.

She tried to muster up indifference but couldn't. Especially as the walls of her office seem to shrink, making the space smaller.

Zurie broke the silence. "I heard you had a hard time getting out of New York. What time did you finally get here?"

"I couldn't get a flight out in time. I had to drive."

That explained the shadows under his eyes. Wait. Had he moved closer or had she? "How was the training in California?"

"Good." Mace definitely stepped closer.

"Thanks for assigning Dean to help out. I really appreciate that." She needed to stop babbling.

"I'm sorry I wasn't here." He dropped his hat onto one of the padded chairs in front of her desk.

"You were busy. You have a lot to do now that you're moving to Reno."

Mace's brow raised a fraction.

Oh... She hadn't meant to say that. Now she'd have to explain how she knew. But she hadn't been snooping around his desk that day. Zurie started to explain.

"I'm not moving to Reno."

"You're not? Why?"

"You know why." Mace walked into her personal

space. "Because of you." He took her hand, wreaking havoc on her concentration.

"You can't."

"Oh, yes, I can."

"No, you are supposed to be a lawyer in Nevada with your family practice, Calderone and Associates. They're expecting you." She could see the question in his eyes about how she knew the name of the practice. She'd looked it up.

"They *were* expecting me, but now they know the practice will have to go on without me. Bolan is where I live. My job as a deputy is here. My home is here. My life is here. And I want you to be a part of it."

For how long? He'd worked hard to get that law degree. Someday he could change his mind and want what his family law firm could offer him.

Zurie shook her head, saying no to him and herself. "My father put Tillbridge in my hands. Not Rina's. Not Tristan's, mine."

"That's a weak argument. You say you can't because of Tillbridge, but I think some of the people in that room, the ones that work for you, your family, would tell you that you don't have to sacrifice yourself for them. And honestly, when your father put this place in your hands, I don't think that's what he intended, either. Tillbridge didn't thrive because of one person. It's here because of family."

Mace cupped her face in his hands. "I want us to

be family. Seeing your face is how I want to start my day, and you're the one I want to come home to at night. I want to visit vineyards with you, watch movies under the stars with you. I want to watch you stick tomato plants or whatever else into the ground, and I want to hear all the names you pick out for them."

As hard as Zurie tried not to imagine it, she couldn't stop herself. What she saw in her mind looked oh so wonderful. Too wonderful to reach for.

Mace glided his thumb across her cheeks, swiping away tears she hadn't realized leaked from her eyes. "And when the time is right, I want us to have kids and choose names for them together. I want to be there when you bring the best of both of us into the world. I want to be by your side, sleep deprived and happy and in awe of what we made together. And that's just the beginning of what can be a wonderful life for us. But you have to want it just as much as I do. I love you, Zurie. But we can't have all that if you won't trust me. If you won't trust yourself enough to love me back, and I won't take halfway. If you want to be with me, it's all in, just like I'm all in for you."

Mace sealed his lips to Zurie's. As a sob fueled by hope and uncertainty escaped from her, he deepened the kiss, chasing her doubts, fighting her fears, stirring up passion.

He wrapped his arms around her, and little by little, the wall she'd built around what she'd given up on most of her life started to crumble. Happiness. It expanded inside her, searching out the place where it belonged. Her heart. But did she even know how to be happy?

The kiss ended too soon. As Mace laid his forehead to hers, the cadence of her unsteady breaths joined his.

He loosened his embrace, and the soft kiss he brushed near her temple made her close her eyes, trying to stop the flow of tears.

Mace gently squeezed her waist. "When you're ready, you know where to find me."

He let go, and by the time she found the courage to open her eyes, Mace was gone.

Chapter Thirty

Mace strode out the front of the guesthouse, fighting the urge to go back for Zurie. But if he did, what would he do? Throw her over his shoulder and carry her away, caveman style? No, he'd said his piece. And he'd done what he'd needed to for Chloe and Tristan's wedding. It was time for him to go home.

He took his phone from the inside pocket of his suit jacket and called Dean. "We're done here. Everyone can head out. And thanks. Drinks are on me at the Montecito next Friday."

"No problem," Dean said. "I'll spread the word about next Friday."

As Mace ended the call, Rina walked out the door of the guesthouse.

"Hey." Rina nudged his arm. "Can you believe it? We pulled it off. Chloe and Tristan's day went perfectly."

Ignoring the viselike feeling around his heart, Mace summoned a smile. "Yep. Just like we planned."

She looked to Scott, walking toward them from the parking lot. "He delivered plates of food to your security guys."

"Thanks for doing that."

"We all really appreciate them being here. Did you grab some food to take home?"

"No, I missed out."

She laughed. "I can definitely rectify that. Most of the leftovers are in my car."

As Scott came closer, Rina headed toward the steps. "A few people are coming by my house tonight to help finish them off. You have to stop by. Can you tell Zurie, too? I lost track of her."

"I don't know where she is."

Scott had reached the bottom of the steps. As Rina walked down them, she paused in taking his outstretched hand. "She's not with you?"

The constraint around Mace's heart grew tighter. "No. Zurie's not with me."

Varying levels of confusion and realization dawned on her face. "Oh… I thought…" Her mouth remained open as if she wasn't sure what to say.

Scott took hold of Rina's hand and gently tugged.

"We should get home so we can put the food in the refrigerator." He gave Mace a bro nod of solidarity. He understood Mace's pain.

Rina slipped her hand from Scott's, walked to Mace and gave him a kiss on the cheek. "If you don't make it by, I'll save you a plate. You can pick it up later."

"Thanks."

As Rina and Scott walked to the car with their arms wrapped around each other's backs, Scott kissed her temple.

The memory of his last kiss with Zurie earlier flitted through his mind. The loss of her followed him as he trekked to the far side of the parking lot. At the truck, he tossed his jacket into the back seat and his tie on top of it.

He glanced toward the guesthouse.

The door opened, and a couple walked out.

Disappointment sat heavy inside him. Yeah, dinner at Rina's house definitely wasn't happening. He was still planning to live his life the best way he could without Zurie, but he needed a minute before he got started on that.

Mace got into the driver's seat and turned the key in the ignition. Before putting the truck in Reverse, he opened the window, needing some fresh air. Glancing behind him as well as in the rearview mirror, he started backing out.

He heard Zurie's voice calling his name. But he

refused to look. *Damn.* He missed her so much, he was hearing her voice.

"Mace!"

Zurie's voice reached him loud and clear through his open window, and he turned, looking for her.

"Mace, wait!" She waved at him from the top of steps. As she hurried down them, she paused to slip off her sandals and flung them aside.

Equal parts of shock and memorization held him in place as she ran toward him down the sidewalk, gray Stetson in hand, her hair streaming behind her, dress clinging to her curves.

He shut off the engine, got out and walked around to the front of the truck.

Zurie slowed to a walk, and he met her halfway.

She was slightly out of breath.

As the wind blew one of her curls over her forehead, he balled his hand in a fist, resisting the urge to smooth it back.

Zurie brushed the strand from her eyes and looked up at him. "You forgot something."

Of course, she was bringing him the hat.

"Thanks." He reached for it.

Zurie held it behind her back and shook her head. "No. You forgot something else."

Before he could ask what, she curved her hand to his nape, urging him to lean in as she lifted on her toes and sealed her mouth to his.

Unable to resist holding her, Mace grasped her by the waist.

When Zurie finally came up for air, his heart was pounding hard and he felt a little light-headed. But that didn't stop him from chasing her mouth for a longer kiss.

Whoops from across the parking lot caught both their attention.

Rina happy danced next to Scott. As she threw her hands in the air in victory, her shouts of *yes* traveled on the breeze.

Zurie's laugh vibrated into Mace.

She'd come to him, but he needed to hear her say why. Mace gave her waist a light squeeze. "What did I forget?"

"Me." She cupped his cheek. "I love you, too. I have to be honest, I'm a little scared. I'm so used to being on my own and handling things myself, but what you promised me in my office a minute ago, I want that with you. If you can be patient with me, I'm ready to go all in."

The trust and love in her eyes made happiness well inside him. Mace bent down, swept up her legs and picked her up his arms. "What took you so long?"

Zurie put the Stetson on her head, freeing up her hands to loop around his neck. "Sorry for being a little late."

"I forgive you, *mi vida*." Mace kissed her, capturing her smile as his own. Zurie was his life…his heart…his love.

* * * * *

For more from Nina Crespo,
keep an eye out for her book in
The Fortunes of Texas:
The Hotel Fortunes continuity,

An Officer and a Fortune

available May 2021 wherever
Harlequin Special Edition books and
ebooks are sold!

SPECIAL EXCERPT FROM

HARLEQUIN

SPECIAL EDITION

When Cory Hall arrives with his—surprise!—infant son, former pro football player Jordan Shaeffer has to devises a new game plan. And Cory finds herself agreeing to be his fake fiancée until they work out a coparenting agreement. Jordan may have rewritten the dating playbook...but will it be enough bring this team together?

Read on for a sneak peek
at the latest book in the Welcome to Starlight series,
His Secret Starlight Baby
by USA TODAY *bestselling author Michelle Major.*

"We need to get our story straight," she reminded him.

His smile faded. "It's best not to offer too many details. We met in Atlanta, and now we have Ben."

She turned to face him, adjusting the lap belt as she shifted. "Your family's not going to question you showing up with a six-month-old baby? Like maybe you would have mentioned it to them prior to now?"

One bulky shoulder lifted and lowered. "I told you we aren't close."

"Your mom not knowing she has a grandchild is a bit more than 'not close,'" Cory felt compelled to point out. "Will she be upset we aren't married?"

"I'm not sure."

Her stomach tightened at his response. “Will she want to have a relationship with Ben after this weekend?”

“Good question.”

“I have a million of them where that came from,” she said. “I don’t even know how your father died.”

“Heart attack.”

“Sudden.” She worried her lower lip between her teeth. There were so many potential potholes for her to tumble into this weekend, and based on the tight set of his jaw, Jordan was in no shape to help navigate her through it. In fact, she had the feeling she’d be the one supporting him and he’d need solace well beyond a distraction.

“Can you answer a question with more than two words?” She was careful to make her voice light and was rewarded when his posture gentled somewhat.

“I suppose so.”

“A bonus word. Nice. I’m sorry about your father’s death,” she said, giving in to the urge to reach out and place her hand on his arm.

Get 4 FREE REWARDS!
We'll send you 2 FREE Books
plus 2 FREE Mystery Gifts.
Their Secret Summer Family
CHRISTINE RIMMER
Her Second Forever
JOANNA SIMS
Harlequin Special Edition books relate to finding comfort and strength in the support of loved ones and enjoying the journey no matter what life throws your way.
FREE
Value Over
$20

Well, Mary faced facts. All mothers thought their sons were nice boys. And just because Estrella Modesto happened to be the kindest mammal on God's green earth didn't mean she didn't have one sour-faced elitist for a son.

"Thirty-seven," Mary replied, unashamed and unwilling to cower under the blazing critique of his bright blue eyes. "My birthday was last week."

"Oh." His face had yet to change. "Happy birthday."

She'd never heard the phrase said with less enthusiasm. He could very well have said, *Happy Tax Day*.

"Evening," a smooth voice said at Mary's elbow. Mary looked up to see a fairly stunning brunette smiling demurely down at them. The waitress was utter perfection in her black vest and white button-down shirt, not a hair out of place in her neat ponytail. Mary clocked her at somewhere around twenty-two, probably fresh out of undergrad, an aspiring actress hacking through her first few months in the Big Apple.

"Evening!" Mary replied automatically, her natural grin feeling almost obscene next to this girl's prim professionalism.

Mary turned in time to catch the tail end of John's appraisal of the waitress. His eyes, cold and rude, traveled the length of the waitress's body.

Nice boy, Estrella had said.

Mary knew, even now, that she'd never have the heart to tell Estrella that nice boys didn't call their dates old and then mentally undress the waitress. Mary was a tolerant person, perhaps too tolerant, but there were only so many feathers one could stuff into a down pillow before it snowed poultry.

"Right," Mary said, mostly to herself, as John and the waitress both looked at her to order her drink. How *nice* of him to pull his eyes from the beautiful baby here to serve him dinner. She turned to the waitress. "I think we need a minute."

Mary took a deep breath. She asked herself the same question she'd been asking herself since she'd been old enough to ask it—which, according to John Modesto-Whitford, was probably about a decade and a half too long. *Can I continue on?* If the answer was yes, if she conceivably could continue on through a situation, no matter how horrible, she always, always did.

PHCBEXP0321

SPECIAL EXCERPT FROM

Read on for a sneak peek at
Flirting with Forever,
the third book in Cara Bastone's charming, heartfelt and irresistibly romantic Forever Yours series. Available January 2021 from HQN!

Mary Trace was one of those freaks of nature who actually loved first dates. She knew she was an anomaly, should maybe even be studied by scientists, but she couldn't help herself. She loved the mystery, the anticipation. She always did her blond hair in big, loose curls and—no matter what she wore—imagined herself as Eva Marie Saint in *North by Northwest*, mysterious, inexplicably dripping in jewels and along for whatever adventure the night had in store. Besides, it had been a while since she'd actually been on a first date, so this one was especially exciting.

"I was expecting someone…younger."

Reality snuffed out Mary's candle. The surly-faced blind date sitting across from her in this perfectly lovely restaurant had just called her *old*. About four seconds after she'd sat down.

Sure, this apparent *prince* wasn't exactly her type either, with his dark hair neatly parted on one side, the perfect knot in his midnight blue tie, the judgmental look in his eye. But she'd planned to at least be polite to him. She'd had some great dates with men who weren't her physical ideal. She certainly didn't point out their flaws to them literally the second after saying hello.

"Younger," Mary repeated, blinking.

The man blinked back. "Right. You must be, what, in your late thirties?"

Mary watched as his frown intensified, his shockingly blue eyes narrowing in their appraisal of her, a cruel sort of humor tipping his mouth down.

A nice boy, Estrella had said when she'd arranged the date. *You'll see, Mary. John is a rare find in a city like this. He's got a good job. He's handsome. He's sweet. He just needs to find the right girl.*

PHCBEXP0321